D0811727

Quarantine

Other Books by Juan Goytisolo
available in English translation

FICTION

Children of Chaos
Count Julian
Fiestas
Island of Women
Juan the Landless
Landscapes after the Battle
Makbara
Marks of Identity
The Party's Over
The Virtues of the Solitary Bird
The Young Assassins

NONFICTION

The Countryside of Nijar and La Chanca
Forbidden Territory: Memoirs 1931-1956
Realms of Strife: Memoirs 1957-1982
Space in Motion

Juan Goytisolo

Quarantine

a novel

Translated by Peter Bush

Dalkey Archive

Originally published in Spanish as *La Cuarentena* by Mondadori España, S.A., 1991.
First American Edition, 1994

Chapter 8 first appeared (in slightly different form) as "Vision of the Day after in Djemaa el Fna" in the *Voice Literary Supplement*, June 1991.

Library of Congress Cataloging-in-Publication Data
Goytisolo, Juan.
[Cuarentena. English]
Quarantine / Juan Goytisolo ; translated by Peter Bush. —1st ed.
I. Title.
PQ6613.O79C813 1994 863'.64—dc20 93-29198
ISBN 1-56478-044-9

The Publishers gratefully acknowledge the support of Spain's Ministry of Culture as well as the Program for Cultural Cooperation between Spain's Ministry of Culture and United States' Universities for this English translation. This publication is partially funded by grants from the National Endowment for the Arts and the Illinois Arts Council.

Dalkey Archive Press
4241 Illinois State University
Normal, IL 61790-4241

Printed on permanent/durable acid-free paper and bound in the United States of America.

A. J. L., in memoriam

Translator's Note

On Ibn Arabi, Asín and the *Miradj*, and Other Islamic References

Born in Murcia, southeast Spain, in 1165, Ibn Arabi became one of the foremost Sufi mystics revered throughout the Islamic world. After living in Seville, he traveled throughout North Africa and the Middle East. On a pilgrimage to Mecca in 1202, he was deeply moved by the sight of the Kaaba, which he saw as a point of contact of the visible and the invisible. He also lived in Konya and Malatya in Anatolia. His most influential work, the *Fusus al-hikam,* describes how a summary of the teaching of twenty-eight prophets was dictated to him in a dream by the Prophet. In his *Futuhat* he explored how man attains different levels of knowledge. Man is engaged in a series of journeys: on the third journey he lives externally with his fellows and internally with God. Ibn Arabi also described the *Miradj,* or the ladder of the Prophet's ascent to heaven. In some versions this journey started in Mecca, in others in Jerusalem. It has been interpreted as a vision that occurred during the Prophet's sleep, an experience affecting body and soul in full consciousness, and a revelation triumphing out of ecstasy. The archangel Gabriel wanders with the Prophet through the gates of each of the seven heavens. Sometimes they visit

Paradise and Hell: the place of the punishment of the damned is on the way between heaven and earth. The Ascension of the Prophet later became a model for the description of the journey of the soul of the deceased to the throne of the divine judge. For Ibn Arabi and the Sufis it symbolized the rise of the soul from the bonds of sensuality to the heights of knowledge. In his *Futuhat,* Ibn Arabi makes a believer and a philosopher journey together but the philosopher only reaches the seventh heaven. The great Spanish Arabist Asín Palacios has described how this Islamic tradition of the Ascension influenced Dante in his composition of *The Divine Comedy,* as a result of *The Book of Mahomet's Ladder* which was translated into Latin from a Castilian text that was in turn translated from the Arabic.

Nakir and Munkar are the names of the two angels who examine and if necessary punish the dead in their tombs. Righteous and sinners are set upright and must state their opinion concerning Mohammed. The righteous will say he is the Apostle of Allah and sinners will have no answer and will be beaten severely by the angels as long as it pleases Allah.

For Sufis *barzakh* is the space between the material world and that of pure spirits. It generally means obstacle and separation and the barrier between hell and paradise. In some versions it denotes the dark substances of the body that will only become light on receiving the light of the spirit.

Fana is the Sufic term for passing away, a stage on the development of the mystic on the path of gnosis: the passing away from the consciousness of the mystic of all things, including himself, even the absence of consciousness of this passing away, and its replacement by the pure consciousness of God.

Macabro is a word that Juan Goytisolo uses to denote a cemetery in Spanish. He is thus reintroducing into modern Spanish a word that was used by medieval writers like the Archpriest of Hita whose language reflected the coexistence of Jewish, Arab, and Christian cultures in Spain before Ferdinand and Isabel. *Macabro* is an adaptation of the Arabic for cemetery, *makbara.* It is the origin of the English word *macabre,* though our dictionaries prefer to opt for an old French derivation which in turn comes from the Arabic. It seems right to translate this as *macabre,* in keeping with the text's reclaiming of the Islamic roots of much that is our ostensibly Christian, European tradition.

Quarantine

1

The writing of a text presupposes the existence of a fine net of relationships binding the different threads that weave within it. Everything converges: outside events, personal experiences, moods, journeys, chance occurrences—all randomly mix with reading, fantasies, images, thanks to an ars combinatoria *of encounters, correspondences, memory associations, sudden illuminations, alternative currents. This writing appeared on my horizon on the eve of the war year. I had already tied its theme to the moment of passage and its eschatology, impelled by the sudden disappearance of a friend and a desire to renew my charmed relationship with her in my writing: skimming and gleaning in* The Divine Comedy, *works by lbn Arabi, books by Asín, different versions of the Prophet's nighttime ascent, Sufi anthologies, Miguel de Molinos's* Spiritual Guide *edited by Spain's greatest living poet, the one she was carrying the day she vanished from my sight. Greatest Master and Seal of the Saints, the Murcian mystic's frequent references to the eye of the imagination and the intermediate realm where spirits reside when they leave their tombs thus became the primary nucleus of a work, the need for which definitively imprinted itself on my mind when I came across the following lines:* "After flying to the in-between world or barzakh, spirits continue in possession of their bodies and the latter adopt the subtle form, the way you see yourself in dreams. For the other universe is a resting place where appearances change continually, like fleeting thoughts in the inner dimension of this world." *The moment I prepared physically to compose the book, I perished. Having moved from short-lived to infinite time, I released myself from myself, at a stroke knew what it was to be light and fluid. On the outside I saw myself as deaf and blind, listless and insentient, attended by a worried kith and kin and a silent, sorrowing wife. I stayed briefly in the room trying not to let my vagary disturb their anguished movements, and waited for the washer to arrive to ensure he performed the rites according to my last wishes. Although the notion of time dissolves, is abolished on the isthmus joining the two worlds, I remember nevertheless how I mentally ordered the chaotic screed of my text while souls roamed and wandered through the period of Quarantine.*

2

Not there as well?

At first only a hint, then spreading out with greater definition, the ambiguous, haunting familiarity of the *Concierto*'s opening bars had subtly permeated the atmosphere.

Were you walking through a spacious hotel lobby? Making a quick ascent cloistered in a comfortable elevator? Or flying at a height of nine thousand meters in an airplane belonging to Turkish Airlines, as you recall once happened, on an internal flight between Erzurum and Ankara? Could they be seeping out of a loudspeaker system cleverly hidden by the functional design of a tourist beehive? From the comfy, padded box loading and unloading silent, satisfied customers? Or from the rows of cabin seats in the tense moments that precede the takeoff and landing of some flying coffin?

How else could one explain the delicate stereophony that seemed to emanate from the blurred boundaries of a space at once oneiric, misty, and unreal? Did it derive perhaps from the distant, shoreless sea the contemplation of which troubled your vision? Was it an effect radiating from the gleam and glitter of the sparkling theater of lights, or from uncannily volatile epiphanies and eclipses? Or was its origin purely luminous, like the aura that sometimes enfolded them when diaphanous, bathed and flooded in light, they quietly, attentively examined the rough, serrated hills with peaks turbaned in clouds or the magnanimous calm of the peaceful, clear sky?

But there were no elevators or hotels, nor even airplanes, she said. Otherwise she'd have come across them when out strolling. She'd been there for some time and hadn't seen or heard any, and she had looked carefully!

She talked with a smile on her lips, as she used to when she regularly brought the typed versions of her texts to his study, and now as then she made as if to take a packet of Gauloises Bleues out of her bag and light up a cigarette, glancing nervously over the shelves of books and magazines for an elusive ashtray, a habit she couldn't break when she spoke to him despite the conspicuous absence from that spot of any pouch, tobacco, or lighter, as if she were condemned to imitating vacuous movements and mannerisms or to obeying a ritual of identification that was patently unnecessary.

Where did that *Concierto*'s pure, intense notes come from, spread over the world of his past like a unique, persistent signature tune to pain and nostalgia? Was it the cruel sound of the blind man's guitar? Or the more jagged version of the trumpeter exulting in rapturous ecstasy?

They had stared at each other equally bewildered, dazed by the growing brilliance of the sphere in which they moved, by the luminous torrent pouring over them, appearing to course like an X ray through marrow and bones, and mutually wondered at the glowing plenitude shining from their faces suddenly thus possessed and transfigured.

She wasn't surprised to see him turn up, she said. Their separation had been so abrupt! She sensed dimly that communication hadn't ceased: that everything she'd wanted to say to him and couldn't had simply been postponed. Now it was all so easy and uncomplicated, even though the aftertaste of past anguish drove her to seek out the futile solace of smoke. So close to him, yet so distant! He listened to her silently as if she were lost in another dream, which left her empty and peaceful despite his restrained, scant affections.

Was it the remorse and emotion at their meeting after such a brutal, undigested absence that made the tears stream from her dry eyes, plunging her into an inner helplessness that was nevertheless imbued by an obscure faith, the other side of regret and sorrow?

In that symbolic gathering where familiar and friendly silhouettes congregated long ago, gradually eroded by the ravages of age and epidemic, why indeed had she and not some other traveler just been brought into the world of subtlety? In her state didn't she crave rigorous remedies, not palliatives? What paths had led her there, as if to a secret lair, through that indefinite expanse of mist and haze?: the *Concierto*'s haunting theme or a more intimate, subterranean sign?

For once she didn't come to consult him or draw on his knowledge, which he ironically described as one-eyed, on some matter in his field, yet not daring to brush the hem of her dress against him, she felt him so distant from her and the silkiness of her bodily forms! There, on the other hand, she could take advantage of her aleatory experience, of her undeserved seniority in a state that had changed initial bewilderment at her lightness into beatitude! She spoke to him in the gentle, benign tone of one no longer reveling in the external, one who remains calm in her inner self, with her fine hair, light blue eyes and the unmistakable dimple in her cheeks, when she smiled gently, half shyly.

They wandered, absorbed in the notes of the *Concierto.*

Lightning and intermittent flashes heightened their brilliance in an empyrean without dawn or dusk, right or left, up or down, both of them encircled by clouds that were ragged, fluid or dense, unsure whether they were cirrus or cumulus, strata or nimbus. Was it all a simulation of the past, as she pretended, or was it a decoy to snare the senses?

They walked along, weightless, hand in hand. You've got forty days left, she'd told him, then you'll change your abode and who knows if we'll see each other again. I'll guide you and show you everything I've seen since I cast off all that is sensuous on the stairway. Listen to the poignant melancholy of the music. They've replaced the blind man's guitar with the trumpet sound which so entrances and captivates you. Don't take off yet, keep a firm foothold. Didn't you once tell me you gave your wife the Miles Davis recording of the *Concierto de Aranjuez* the first time you went out with her?

3

You had poked your head or what you thought was your head out of dreams or clouds unable to sustain such a steadfast belief in a mirror of mercy and were witness to the implacable spectacle of the diaspora of entire nations, thousands upon thousands of blind, muzzled creatures, fleeing from stony, blackened lands, past ashen woods and trickling rivers. Was it the threatening initiation of the ill-fated millennium that scattered peoples to the four winds in noisy disarray? Were they looking for refuge in that sea of thick, compacted shadows, in flight from the voracious, cremating Gehenna of nuclear weaponry or chemical warfare?

You made swift progress across the devastated landscape and your car headlights fleetingly lit up miserable, bemused specters or shadows, hobbling through the dark shadows on the road, gripping a bottle of cheap liquor, a glint of terror lurking in the deep fissures of their eyes.

Where were they going and who were they running from?

Had the threats been realized of shriveled bodies, liquefied brains, ruined cities, mutilated limbs of countless victims strewn over seas of blood? Or could they be bands of the possessed or wraiths driven on by the fear of imminent punishment?

They travel the Earth cursing their dead ideals and putrefied dogmas, she said, as if she'd read his thoughts.

The car was the old DKW from your childhood, perhaps a rickety, grimy Lada that seemed to move along stealthily, and worryingly independent. Thronging bands, drunken and hirsute, surged out of the blackness at every turn spewing unsavory curses down upon you both, murky utterances expressed in infinitives. Some ran panic-stricken, like hares caught out on nighttime forays; others rushed like moths into the heat and destruction of the flame. Then you had to steer to avoid them, zigzagging over the pockmarked tarmac, with a skill and timing that kept you on edge. Despite its vintage age and wheezing, reluctant engine, the vehicle slipped along ever more impetuously, swerving miraculously round the groups of hapless wanderers weighed down by their chattels and a surly mass of clinging offspring.

You glimpsed massive migrations, corpses that had been violently exhumed, grandiose statues knocked from their pedestals and hammered to smithereens, doctrinal treatises and political credos thrown on the fire, piles of burning bones, renamed streets and squares, bodies garotted and reduced to ash, houses razed as symbols of ignominy, musty, faded, emaciated figures, a raggle-taggle of cheats, flocks led by wolves rather than shepherds, not a grain of truth, no mounds of dust, no mountains of straw.

Was it then they got close to the vision of helicoidal floors, astronomical heavens, circles of the mystic rose, sublunary worlds derived from the informing virtue lit up and inflamed by the real sun? Or were they, as he'd read before taking this path, mere fantasy and deception?

Don't be impatient, don't rush. Although for once I anticipated what you experienced and learned through your senses, my own eyes have seen none of that, not even on the programs on the closed-circuit Television. These people are discovering, as your fellow countryman noted long before we came into the world, that they're not antisocial, depraved, criminal, miscreant, lumpen or hooligan elements as depicted in their regimes' propaganda but deluded adepts of masters who "ride on the winds of deceitful theories, give stones for bread, leaves for fruit and as real food insipid earth mixed with poisonous honey." Now in their rage they burn the idols they once worshiped and curse the futile sacrifice of whole generations.

You fell asleep at the steering wheel and dreamt of a huge warehouse packed with paintings, portraits, statues, and busts of the Guide, Savior and Father of the Fatherland, solid, swollen-headed, macrocephalic, the whole range of postures and attributes delivered up by the stunted inspiration of artificers as servile examples of their well-paid constipation: on horseback in a gendarme's kepi brandishing a blazing sword! pointing to a radiant future with the solemn, emphatic gesture of a policeman directing the traffic! dressed in top hat and tails, like a magician or conjurer! dinner-jacketed, in starched collar and bow tie, a greasy Gardel of a dancing-master! painted with the pensive blue eyes and bushy brows of a hypnotist! Einsteinly meditative in his scientific researcher's laboratory! caressing a fair-haired girl, all innocent smiles and heavenly charms! leaning over the map of a battlefield, waving a wizardly forefinger at the weak point in the enemy positions! Thousands of portraits unhooked from official centers and offices, an infinity of statues hurriedly withdrawn from parks and avenues, bust after warlike bust forced into inactivity, glorious heads with dusty eyelids and nostrils, occupying acres of derelict warehouses and hangars, overwhelming you with the infinitely multiplying effect of their flashing eyes and bizarre poses!

A few well-known silhouettes roam around dwarfed by the forest of stone pedestals and plinths, bent double under the weight of fossilized flattery, their defense of a yokel's belches reproduced on the statues as pithy, profound truths. The loudspeakers in this sinister shelter relentlessly broadcast poems and eulogies to King Joe and Maurice, a dolorous Pasionaria and Fidelio and in vain they try to escape from them, floundering with clumsy, tired gestures.

(Are you dreaming, are you still dreaming?)

Hard-pressed, insectile multitudes, in perpetual ferment, tear down, burn, destroy, pulverize the symbols of the Genius, burn their recruitment certificates and Party cards.

The Lada (or is it the old DKW?) zigzags wildly, dodging a crowd of sleepwalkers, and seems to levitate over the road that is created and unmade as it goes along, erasing itself from the ground as if it were a mirage.

Don't be afraid, she says. We haven't moved. You haven't acclimatized yet. I had the same experience at first, but after feeling helpless in the dark, thinking I was lost, I suddenly discovered I was strong and serene, and had never foreseen such happiness.

(You're together in a pergola or rustic arbor surrounded by clouds and she mechanically goes through the motion of lighting a nonexistent cigarette, realizes her anachronism, and finally smiles along with you in that gentle, jovial complicity that bound you.)

Quick, the binoculars!

You focus them on a narrow coffin of flames, a gaggle of naked men and women, their eyelashes sewn up with barbed wire, an upside-down tree with heavenly roots and topsy-turvy branches, a snake as long as a month on the road.

A lady with a parasol, wearing a dress of lilac organdy, lace flounces and big bows, necklaced with glass beads, medallions and cameos, with white stockings, high-heeled shoes, a spangled, imitation diamond buckle on the instep, is strolling between the mossy balustrades and pots of hydrangeas.

(Who is it? Haven't you seen her somewhere before?)

Suddenly you realize you've lost contact with your investigators. The discovery alarms you but her limpid, watery gaze has an immediately calming effect.

Time here no longer rushes by. And so you'll see no clocks, nor anything similar. There they talk of days, months and years; but one of our pauses can seem an eternity in the middle of the interrogation. They only have to connect the video to summon up incidents and episodes from your past!

(The vision from the luminous, unreal air shuttle merges with scenes of turmoil and panic, a bitter tumult of voices, a slow, persistent drizzle of flakes of fire.

Was your night of solitude a living death?)

4

Like an evil genie posted on the vertical escarpment of the Mount which according to the Hadith is probably one of the gardens of Eden, or perched on one of the minarets adjacent to the mausoleum of the woman inflamed by Pure Love, you survey the vast panorama of domes, tombs, mansions, Sufi lodges, Koranic schools which you tamed years ago with your natural tendency to burn shoe leather, gently bathed now in milky moonlight, majestic, peaceful and quiet, its inhabitants sleeping in the pantheons amid a dense silence suffused with tranquillity and kindness. Are you one of the pleiad of wandering shades, given over to reminiscence and nostalgia during quarantine? Do you fly and glide with them from the mosque and lookout towers of the Citadel to the mounds and Dervish convents of Mukattam?

You slice through the fresh, invigorating air like a kite or a bird, surprised at your own agility and lightness, levitating over flagstoned patios decorated with Koranic verses, tombs topped by stelas, porticos with baskets of flowers and evergreen plants, tiled cenotaphs with Kufic inscriptions. A refined instinct or the secret presence of an organ endowed with the power to hover and steer grants you instant weightlessness, ecstatic inebriation, a flight skimming over tombs covered in palm fronds, dishes of seeds and bowls of water, the fearful immobility of someone perceiving himself in a sacred arena of sadness and inner contemplation, which is nevertheless steeped in a mysterious, reassuring pity.

You are alone, nobody accompanies you on your nocturnal wandering through the deserted city. You have traversed the stages of passive aridity, darkness, anguish, contradictions, continual repulsion, inner helplessness, and resilient despair mentioned in the *Spiritual Guide* you gave her; are you now pure faith, without image, shape, or face, immersed in your own void and returned to your kernel? Why have your investigators abandoned you under the vaulted ceiling of the tunnel of rose-colored stone, and not even taken the trouble to adjust the stone slab hiding the steep, narrow stairs? Is it a careless slip or a desire on their part to put you to the test, granting you an interlude in which to reconsider and remember?

How can you strike up a dialogue over two thousand kilometers with the conclave of phantoms from your childhood and family? A mother cut down and suddenly flung into the void, a father lost, then lingeringly reclaimed in your humble hideaways in the medina, grandparents held by you in the merciless swath of harsh light before the Great Resurrection foretold, always associated in your memory and consciousness with images of churches and a God of stone, chimerical, suppurating Christs, bleeding Dolorosas, barren ceremonies, futile communions, dead feelings! Must you yet return to disturb their ashes and stir their bones, to expose their shades to a despairing picture of human misery and fratricidal hatred, the bitter fruit of seed sown in childhood? Treacherous memories of peace, love, maternal happiness that also besieged your double or dubbed version on the eve of the migration of his soul! Didn't you expiate all that in a small café in the Alcazaba for the derisory cost of a thimbleful of maashun? Nevertheless, insistently they reappear, like the latent image on a plate or film during processing, blurred and shapeless at first, discernible and well-defined later, out of the amorphous mass of specters, past a long trail of drawbridges, huge, arduous obstacles, plummeting slopes, skirting the red, incandescent mansions of trial and expiation: she's in the full bloom of youth, photographed in loving profile or on a tennis court, racket in hand; he's as you remember him in his last years, aged and shriveled by his widowerhood and illness, weighed down by scientific enterprises that so painfully aborted. Haven't they suffered indescribable anguish and intolerable distress by leaving their secure haven to take even the briefest look at the ocean of the world, in response to your call? Is there silent reproach in their eyes or tacit gratitude at your longing for a now impossible dialogue as they fade into the mist and go back to their parallel beds in the distant family pantheon? Your delightfully crazy grandmother (did she lose her senses by dint of a theophany, as Ibn Arabi argued, is she an unreasonable creature of reason?) and her husband (forever hiding behind his newspaper dating from the siege of Stalingrad?), though they lie in another cemetery, they also join the cortege but don't revile you because you've poked their bones around, exposed to view what should remain secret till the Final Day of Forgiveness. Their silhouettes become transparent in the diaphanous night of the macabre, of cenotaphs adorned with Koranic verse and witnesses topped by turbans of stone, striated domes, dervish shrines, dovecotes, the mausoleum of the Sultan of the

Beloved with a reader of the Koran reciting the sacred stanzas of the Book. Once more you glide across the serene sky, rocked by a wind that seems to stir the glowing embers of the stars, over an area of hovels and inhabited pavilions, deserted alleyways, noctivagous shadows, the dense breathing and pulsating of a million residents crouching down, impish devils on the loose, tombs of sheiks, small freshly painted houses of pilgrims to Mecca, minarets towering like sentinels over the sleeping community.

(She has moved away from you, and without her precious guidance, you suddenly feel parched and helpless.)

Some Nubians in white djellabas, woollen sashes artfully entwined around their heads, are diligently, stealthily preparing the street awning where hours later the relatives of the deceased will bid farewell to the forty days of mourning, amid gentle sighs and leisurely sips of tea.

5

Contrary to legend they weren't repulsive, sinister-looking blacks, with disfigured faces and voices resounding like thunder, nor did their eyes flash in the darkness of the vault like blinding lightning.

Their hammer! Didn't they wield a club that was so heavy it couldn't even be lifted by the combined effort of all humanity?

If there were one, she hadn't spotted it anywhere!

Didn't she receive seven terrible blows to the skull whenever her reply didn't satisfy them?

It all happened so differently from the way it had been depicted!

Didn't their questioning perhaps harass her into silence, make her a prey to guilt and terror?

No, none of it was remotely like the prisons of the Inquisition. There weren't methods of torture like the rack, the water or electric treatment, the bathtub or goad, only a space, whose oppressive narrowness had been transmuted into something immense and imprecise where their words vibrated like a very soft whistle that was impossible to locate.

Could she see them?

Rather she caught a glimpse of them amid the haze and, after each anagnorisis, felt resplendent and serene, cured of her faintness, anguish, and insecurity.

Their voices!

Nakir's resounded grave and diaphanous, no blurred edges, despite the rather defective quality of the amplification. Munkar's revealed a playful tone, as if nourished by subterranean irony or consummate knowledge of human weakness. They hadn't come there to read her the riot act or put her to the test. They were aware of her words and deeds, knew her works from A to Z. They had even taken the trouble to read shelf after shelf of commentaries and doctoral theses by specialists, both the crude and the subtle varieties! Not forgetting her enemies' slanderous pamphlets. What an insulting collection! Munkar chuckled. After that, how could she still be accused of erroneous, heretical, vile, scandalous, ill-written propositions? Surrounded by the detritus of mean, miserable times, as filled with straw as they were short on vital juices, her life made text at least had the merit of contagious passion, the salutary power of dissonant imagination.

Was that all?

What else could she say if, as she heard their words, she felt that one of them, if not both, set her alight with a candle, a very gentle fire, a fire filling her with joy, ablaze everywhere, transforming the seclusion and silence that come after the passage into sweetness!

And, what then?

She woke up: she was looking at an enormous empty screen, as if the projectionist had interrupted the film of his own volition or to obey an order from a superior. Then Ibn Arabi had appeared to her, and she recognized him at once by the singular beauty that he radiated, with his manuscript of *The Epistle of the Human Tree and Four Birds.* He invited her to follow him, seeing her stripped bare and ready, light and revived. She fell asleep again and in her dreams heard him mumble: I drank the inheritance of milky perfection.

(He surveyed the Square, the concrete, seminal space of the Square, absorbed in the leisurely bustle of the crowds, the hazy little clouds of people that formed and dispersed on its perimeter like frayed, footloose cumulus. How many days, months or years had he stood there in his watchtower, deep in thought, absent-mindedly answering his friends' questions, from within the blissful tranquillity of his inner silence?)

6

So that's what it was! she cried, releasing herself from her body that was immobilized on the flight of stairs, pleasantly surprised by the quick end to the searing pain down her left side, the predicted heart attack that had finished her brother and mercilessly punished the whole family, already released from herself and her image as a casually dressed youngster, one hand gripping the rail as if she had looked for help to stop herself falling at the moment of passage, immediately adapted to her subtle form, the invisible owner for a few hours of the entire collection of books, furniture, souvenirs, and photographs that marked her life, all the authors from her Spanish courses that she re-read, buried herself in to translate him, and the typewriter with an unfinished page of her study of Sor Juana.

My brother's disappearance had left me vulnerable, I couldn't get used to that, and I was full of harsh self-recriminations for being unable to foresee it, for not catching the telltale slip of the tongue or the tiny pointers to its existence until that irrevocable, abrupt separation plunged me into a well of darkness, devastated by my total ignorance of this lightness, without a glimmer or inkling of our transcendence, once the anguished constrictions of the night of solitude have passed.

In none of my periods of breakdown and collapse, brief rift with the world, escape from all mental dissipation behind the walls of a psychiatric hospital, had I felt like this: bare, denied, annihilated, nothing to cling to after my amorous failures beyond the small light I sometimes found in your eyes and the overpowering urge to drink, to gain the illumination brought by intoxication, to come to your study slightly tipsy! I did not then know that the enlightenment of wine revealed my blind search for a purer form of inebriation. And that I discovered, thanks to you and the spiritual universe of the Sufis. I couldn't stop smoking, piling the cigarette butts into the mortar, stinking your room up, and I saw your sadness when you poured out my drinks, rightly fearing the shipwreck of my intellect, my total detachment from life and its sociable ways. I didn't know my brother had simply preceded me into the state of lightness! I wallowed in grief, felt dizzy before the abyss. I can't continue working with you, I told you. Find a more suitable, well-balanced person! That night, when I felt your help, I dreamed that with a candle you gently spread to every part of me a fire that I welcomed and enjoyed, like a sweet, spicy dish.

In the dialogue we sustained, I found it difficult to distinguish the questioner from the answerer. Who is "says," who is "I say"? Who talks in the masculine and who in the feminine? Isn't the distinction between the sexes negated in the zone of subtlety? What can we do about the rules of grammar? Why do we refer to He and not She?

She laughed, laughed repeatedly while she played with the gold chain that appears in her photograph, surveying with you, from her lookout post in the clouds, the myriad shades also waiting for the end of quarantine, serenely trusting to forgiveness and hope.

7

Can you see all right? she asks. If the picture's snowy or blurred, you can adjust it with the remote control.

In the sepulchral dark where you levitate outside space and time, once you've climbed the steps of inner bareness to the zone of blessed peace, not realizing what you're doing, whether you're contemplative or not, whether you do good works or not, unconcerned or worried, in step with the Guide, by anything sensuous, you passively absorb the succession of cruel images on the screen in the restful void of your own silence.

In turn you contemplate

men and women, mouths ripped at the corner, eyes and ears pierced by sharp-pointed arrows, hanging upside-down by the backs of their knees, bitten by snakes,

an executioner, lifting a huge rock in both hands, pulverizing the skull of some poor wretch and, not granting a moment's respite, returning to attack the miraculously restored head, endlessly repeating the grisly, systematic torture,

the waves of a river of boiling blood against which a reprobate is struggling to reach the shore where his exterminator lies in wait and cruelly slots pebbles like burning embers into his gasping mouth, forcing him to swim back into the swell so as to renew his torment, a tubular stove, in the flames of which naked men and women shoot up and down like incinerated wood shavings, impelled to the top as if blown by bellows and then flung to the bottom and back, to a chorus of shrieks and cries of terror,

swollen, convulsed creatures, ceaselessly vomiting through eyes, mouths, noses, and ears the sinuous tongues of fire penetrating their rectal orifices,

an immense ocean of fire, subdivided into seventy lesser seas, on the beaches of each one, towering incandescent, a purple city of seventy thousand dwellings storing in turn seventy thousand fiery coffins of writhing, weeping men and women bitten by snakes and scorpions.

Are they photographs of paintings by Bosch or color reproductions of the Doré engravings that startled you as a child? Had not the Florentine perhaps been inspired by boldly internalized visions of *The Book of the Ascent* when he composed his *Comedy?*

If the subject matter oppresses or disturbs you, she says, you can switch channels.

But the program begins again, you're not sure whether deliberately or through technical error, when the tape finishes and in the luminous flickering penumbra, the screen is filled with shots of reprobates, mouths ripped and eye-sockets transfixed by arrows, hanging by the backs of their knees, bitten by snakes.

Oh, comme ils sont emmerdants! says the Lady with the Parasol. Ils ne peuvent pas s'offrir comme tout le monde une antenne parabolique?

She seems to have vanished, without trying to light her nonexistent cigarette or even to arouse you with the pool of light from her bright eyes.

Perhaps your investigators are preparing to submit you to some severe, summary examination?

Sensations of the opaque and the diaphanous, the crass and the subtle precede the eruption of fresh vistas of harsh guards, flame-throwing looks, cities consumed by an inner fire, mansions for purging and pain designed from a delirious desire for symmetry:

a funnel-shaped abyss or the inverted shape of a cone descending to the center of the Earth through nine levels or circles, punishment and prison for each corresponding category of perverse souls, fiery harpoons, clusters of victims, snakes slipping into mouths and out of anuses after ripping intestines, eyeless creatures in rivers of sulphur, men with bellies full of reptiles, women hanging by their hair or by their breasts from red-hot hooks, monstrous dog-headed, pig-bodied beasts, tongues cut by incandescent scissors, racked by thirst forced to drink glasses of molten metal, lanced and whipped by instruments of fire, souls squeezed and pulled apart by a rebel angel bellowing in pain stretched on his rack.

Suddenly, to an English commentary, images of a blonde girl, dazzling smile, inviting breasts, and mother-of-pearl skin, rinsing her thick tresses under the shower, swooning in narcissistic if not orgasmic bliss over the beautifying qualities of a popular brand of shampoo.

Have they interrupted the program on the television network with an advertising slot?

While you wonder, bemused, whether the multinationals are also active in your new terrain, you think you can hear Munkar's mocking laugh in the pitch-dark.

8

He was in his center, his dwelling and delight, at the heart of a world palpitating with life, sought out at once by smells, gestures, touches, the taste of brochettes and bowls of harira, conscious of the uniqueness and diversity of each one of its particles, of its radical equality with the protean mass of bodies object of its magnetic power, pity, or desire, a shared destiny assumed in the nakedness of birth and passage, bunches of human beauty beyond words, of brilliance suddenly eclipsed.

Was it perhaps old age or exhaustion that had gradually led him away from the compelling territory of the halqa? The melancholy feeling that in his writing he had exhausted its original, diaphanous luxuriance? The truth is one day he gave up grazing among the rings of people, his instinctive, fertile nomadism, to settle down and watch the spectacle from the corner of his café. Did he need to impose a distance between himself and everyone else or impose a distance in relation to himself? Was he suddenly, acutely aware of his precariousness, of the inexorable obliteration of everything he nostalgically perceived as still near but already beyond reach? A mere Peeping Tom, at any rate, by the side of the fleeting whirl of passersby twisting between the stalls, awnings, portable stoves, plastic mats with their entire range of proliferating, assorted merchandise. Was the space whose flame had enlightened him in times of blissful plenitude also condemned to disappear? Was the fruitful theater of light and shadow, of daily dramas and play-acting that nourished his life and creative, voracious appetite to be mercilessly swept away?

And he went one step further: he withdrew to his house adjacent to the Square and, from his lookout point on the flat terrace roof, his greedy eyes were happy to store away scenes of the crowd, life not yet annihilation, ifná or fana, his binoculars homing in on Saruh's sturdy, perfectly shaved cranium, the ring around Cherkaui and his trained pigeons, shadows, more shadows from scudding little clouds, blown along and scattered by a light breeze around the ghost of the last jugglers, child acrobats, doctors endowed with innate knowledge, reciters of spells, fortune-tellers, story-tellers, snake charmers, smiling gnaua dancers. A very delicate thread still joined him to that universe of specters directly threatened by a steamroller the roar from which was gradually drowning out the hum of voices, and even the muezzins' call to prayer from the minarets by the Square.

It was on that afternoon of January 17 when, shivering, wrapped up against the north wind from the gleaming snow-covered mountains, he spotted the first cart-load of corpses reaching its bare, deserted perimeter. They arrived without mules or drivers from Bab Ftuh and Semmarin, Riad Ez-Zitun and Mohammed el-Khamis with a timing that was impeccably synchronized, as if guided by remote control or driven by some supernatural force. He began to count them, first singly and then by the dozen as they converged on the center and emptied out their loads, huge piles of stiff or dislocated bodies, mouths half-opened as if to let out a final cry, eyes terrified out of their sockets. No pious souls had dutifully washed and wrapped them in shrouds, closed their eyelids, plugged their ears and nostrils with cotton, tied their feet and jaws with string, decorously crossed their hands over their chests or leaned them to the right according to holy precept. Little by little, the space of the halqa and bartering traders had changed as in the legendary baptism of the Square, into an assembly of corpses whose number was growing at the mechanical, regular rate of mass-production lines in a large factory. Was it a violent evocation of *Night and Fog* forever engraved on his memory, in all its naked horror? His binoculars briefly framed a succession of raw images of shackled bodies, bullet holes in the napes of necks, chests riddled by machine-gun fire, backs hacked to pieces by bayonets, faces set by toxic gases or decompressant bombs into grimaces of unspeakable pain. Only then did he notice the first still silent waves of the flood.

A stream of blood, as if overflowing from a large lake or reservoir, was slowly advancing from the streets near the Bank of the Maghreb and the Post Office, spreading, gently turning the ground red between the human pyramids piled high by the constant scramble of carts. *Who could give voice even with random words / to so much bloodshed and so much injury / even with language turned inside out?* he recalled. The flow was visibly rising, now covering the car park and the terrace of the Glacier café, and getting higher by the minute. From which immense web of veins and arteries was it pouring? From the poverty-stricken people of Ben Suda? demonstrators machine-gunned down on the streets of Oran? humiliated, insulted inhabitants of the poor districts of Cairo? the martyrs of Sabra and Chatila? mothers caught shopping by the savage bombing of Beirut? adolescent stone-throwers from Kafr Malik? exterminated villagers from Halabja? children trapped in the inferno of El Chatti? Or was it simply the beds of the Tigris and the Euphrates gushing into the Medina of the Seven Holy Men, engulfing gardens, markets, avenues, and cafés? He looked at the Kutubia and discovered a scorched, blood-soaked shirt waving from the pole of the flag that had been hoisted during prayers. What angry angel or messenger of death could have planted it there? Stationed in his fragile watchtower, he had no need of binoculars to see the threatening swell of the tide as it flooded the bazaars opposite and swept away their goods and merchandise. Was it now submerging the basement of the Hôtel de France, was it turning unchecked the corner on towards Riad Ez-Zitun? He listened to the flood surging along the narrow passageway and saw it stain red the entrance to the Eden cinema, rushing like a drove of bewildered oxen through the labyrinth of alleyways that led to his house. The crash, the crash of waters bursting through the barriers of a dam, climbed brutally and threateningly up the walls of the rooms. Had the city suddenly been emptied of all its inhabitants? Did no one else see that bloody deluge? He attuned his ears to catch the cries and wailing, waited in vain for some labial sign of life. The thick liquid had burst into the porch from the street, was pouring into the patio, covering the potted plants and the little fountain! Did no one living there notice what had happened? Come on, quickly, fetch buckets and cloths, make a dam, stop that blood from coming up the stairs. Can't you see it's going to get into the library and soak the books? Save at least the drafts and notes of this text, the Islamic, Christian, and Hebrew mystics, the works of Dante and Ibn Arabi, the *Spiritual*

Guide, The Book of the Ascent! Don't let it cover and erase the expression of human understanding and feeling, don't let the words of substance be destroyed! Was he talking to himself? Was any fearful soul listening to him? But already everything was red and from the crimson sky and its hostile coalition of purple clouds rained a similar downpour of blood, drops bursting like ripe fruit over the precarious signs he had traced, the scattered manuscript pages of his work that was unfinished and drowned forever. He had time only to open the book of poems he was holding and read *Gently walk the Earth, it will soon be your grave,* before being sucked into the whirlpool eddying towards the plethora, the corpses, and the exterminating angel in the Square.

9

Was it the premonition of their fragility that made him rush like an anxious, harassed collector to review the prints of the most beautiful places he knew before they disappeared forever from sight through the actions of his Creditor? Or was it the disruption of age, evident in his clumsy gestures and haltering movements as he tuned into the news program, when he saw his old beloved cities rise up before his memory, now transformed into huge piles of scrap metal and black craters according to the jubilant chorus of barking newshounds? Haroun al-Raschid's capital lit up by the glow from the bombing raids like a familiar, beloved Christmas tree! Enemies surprised like cockroaches when a bedroom light is switched on and crushed, as they scatter frantically, by the righteous fury of the exterminator!

He decided to flee that intolerable atmosphere, the silent reproaches on so many solemn faces, the guiltiness he rejected but that corroded him nevertheless. He got into his runt of a car and foot hard on the accelerator headed towards the snowcapped mountains along a road that twisted between prickly pears and almond trees in blossom. Could the rare passersby, crouching villagers, and shepherd boys frozen like scarecrows be the pebbles sown by his clapped-out, asthmatic yellow car as it careered along? What else could they think except that he was on his way to his regular appointment in Samarra?

He reached the small medina with its ocher-pink walls and parked in the empty car park. The strapping lad in vest and red breeches who usually welcomed the tourists getting off their luxury coaches wasn't in his customary place by the open doorway between the buttresses of the wall, the porters' little carts slumbered on the shady path to the entrance hall, the once animated souvenir shops displayed their sickly selection of useless trinkets and postcards. He filled in the form the receptionist handed him and disappeared into the deserted gardens along tiled passageways that crossed over plots planted with bamboo, bananas, and exotic shrubs, a succession of secluded patios adorned with small fountains. Watery gatherings of turtles, hundreds of empty rooms, leisurely servants moving about like furtive specters—the whole area belonged to him! A band of hungry cats, with bloodshot, luciferous eyes, escorted him to the door of his refuge.

Then, minutes, hours later, lying back in a deck chair by the unusually solitary pond, he experienced intensely, uniquely, time's hectic pace, its frenzied devouring of things and creatures: a keen twilight breeze insistently swaying the slender trunks of the copra palms, shaking and ruffling their haughty plumes, binding and unraveling sinister congregations of clouds. Magnolia leaves and bark fell on the disturbed light over the water, on absurd, inane armchairs, the ridiculous decor of a suddenly obliterated world. The arrival of a peacock irately displaying its feathers filled him with terror. Had the flight taken to Simorg been transmuted into nightmare?

And he fled, fled back across vast tracts of precipitous mountains, in search of new hiding places, more secret refuges, convinced he was nothing, could do nothing, was worth nothing, pursued by somber, ephemeral images: vistas of hamlets huddled around their mosques, farmsteads perched like eagles' nests, tiny flocks of sheep intermingling with visions of nuclear winter, acid rain, forests reduced to cinder, devastated landscapes.

He stopped his car by a crossroads and deciphered the blurred inscription on the poster:

DEAD END

Could he reverse the car?

The road markings had faded behind him! His car had been stripped, was burning as if hit by an enemy rocket!

In that geography of desolation he picked out a giant tree, whose shade seemed to offer blissful consolation amid the dismal paths across that scorched earth.

Was it the Lotus of the Terminus?

She was waiting for him at its foot, disputing fiercely with the Lady with the Parasol.

10

She had traversed the parched wastes of the soul, endured persistent desolation, suffered the spiritual torture and inner torments prescribed by the mystic and, at the end of the tests, had been born anew, slender, delicate, spriglike, levitating in the hazy area where you find your own graceful, oneiric weightlessness.

As I cannot be your Beatrice, she says in that tone of jocular complicity you once shared, if you want to visit Gehenna you'd better enlist the services of some agency. Ask them to show you their illustrated brochures and schedules of excursions and they'll provide you with a polyglot hostess!

She laughs again, just like the old days when she waited for you outside the lecture hall and you went off to continue the discussion of the Archpriest and *La Celestina* on the park benches in Washington Square or seated in a cafeteria near the Department. As usual, she was smoking her Gauloises Bleues.

Wasn't there a childish morbidity, an unhealthy fascination in the poet's urge to identify acquaintances and enemies in the infernal circles of reprobates? Take the case of Filippo Argenti in Canto 8! The description of his torment could not be more graphic yet our fine friend, rather than pitying the wretch, exults in the spectacle.

You both glide swiftly along as if on a ski slope and she takes her annotated copy of the *Comedy* out of her bag. What a pity he hadn't included in his lectures a comparative study of Dante and the *Miradj* of Ibn Arabi, and deepened the furrow ploughed by Asín! The Seal of the Saint's conception of divine forgiveness doesn't concur with the bard's one iota nor does he share the other's unfeeling harshness. Can you imagine Ibn Arabi writing these lines: *"Master," I said, "before we leave that lake / my heart yearns / to see the criminal sink into that pit"?* I know we can't judge a work of the beauty and magnitude of the *Comedy* on the basis of such detail, but we can judge its author!

You are in what looks like a travel agency decorated with flashy posters of reproductions of Bosch and watercolors by Gustave Doré. You can make out on the counter the price list for various individual itineraries and sightseeing tours. Ah, pour ça je peux vous offrir un prix tout à fait exceptionnel, says the Lady with the Parasol, a prey to her telephones. Elle est justement en promotion! When she hangs up, she's still answering several lines simultaneously: Si per domani . . . Please wait a moment . . . D'accord, je vous réserve les places dans un instant. . . . After a few exchanges intercut with sighs and laments, Oh, je n'en peux plus! she picks up her faxes and takes a quick look at the computer screen.

Excusez-moi, she says as she finally turns to face you. Je suis toute à vous!

You look to her to ask for help, but find that you are alone, she has disappeared.

From behind her mask of makeup, stylized eyebrows and lashes, eye shadow, face powder, and aggressively scarlet heart-shaped lips, the Lady seems to realize you're upset and opens out her fan with a flirtatiously seductive flourish.

Ne vous inquiètez pas! Une visite privée avec guide en vous éclairera davantage!

11

You dream that you're in a huge waxworks museum like the ones you visited years ago in Paris and Los Angeles. You advance down a luxuriously carpeted corridor whose side walls display a succession of scenic shots from *The Garden of Earthly Delights* and representations of the underworld by the illustrator of the *Comedy.* The face of the hostess pointing your way has no defined features and she treats you, or so you feel, rather condescendingly. Her erudition palls, and you entertain yourself by examining the motionless figures on the panels, trying to pick out the well-known faces. One of the impaled bodies is still twitching and seems stoically to be enduring the pain and smiling through gritted teeth. The explanations pouring from the megaphone are gradually orchestrated by the sound of anvils, gusts of wind, howls of anger.

These nobly dressed characters, in a halo of virtue and sanctity, are Ibn Taymiyya, Torquemada, and Menéndez Pelayo: they are suffering no torture: no boiling sulphur, perpetual devouring, or red-hot harpoons. Their torment is more refined, more acute. In the circles of glory they contemplate those their narrowmindedness condemned as heretics, zendiks, Kaffirs, and other abominable deviations: noble Ibn Arabi, Greatest Master and Seal of the Saints; Al Hallajj, Al Bisthami, and Suhravardi; the Shadili, the illumined, and the quietists; the sublime Miguel de Molinos; Don José María Blanco. What a wonderful lesson they're being given! They conceived of paradise or xanna as the exclusive club of a small clique and ignored Rahma, the Unique One's limitless mercy!

(Who's talking? Is it the uniformed hostess or her voice, hidden for some reason, in the furtive anonymity of the shadows?

Are the figures you can make out on the side walls also part of the intermediate world where spirits are given a subtle body, like the one we see in our dreams?)

Some vaguely familiar people whet your curiosity. You distance yourself from the others and scrutinize, but can't successfully identify, a woman laughing to herself, as if she's celebrating the success of a spell or secret intrigue. On her left, a popular self-publicist, rival to Midas, transforms all he touches into a philosophical treatise. Other inconsistent little figures work themselves up in the offices of a house in darkness, disguised as sea-wolves.

Come on, she says in a friendly bantering tone. Don't tell me you've now become as petty and maniacal as Dante himself! What on earth do you care if an obese, alcoholic Valkyrie of a Lithuanian is eternally condemned to write her apocryphal reader's notes in the dungeons of her faded empire? Haven't you manufactured the occasional pseudo text at some time in your life?

(The people you're looking at, you realize in your confusion, belong to the visible world and their presence in the museum is either absurd or mere allegory. Who included them among the shades: your vengeful imagination or a Munkar leg-pull?)

That one's a charlatan jack of no trades! the hostess cuts in, after pointing a finger at the self-publicist. He knows he won't get into the history of ideas, of the novel, drama, or essay, even though he's spread his seed disastrously over all those fields! We might aptly say about him: "Shoemaker, to your shoes," but as he's ignorant even of this worthy trade, out of politeness, let's just say to him, "Gentleman, to your gentles!"

(Isn't the Seminarian oozing in boils, his mouth enclosed in a kind of sheath or muzzle, simmering in the stench of his own slaver, a creature out of one of your own books?

Why does the woman insist on showing you his stinking, charred mass?)

You want to escape from the museum, rid yourself of the burden of that guided tour, but she begs you not to wake the hostess with any rash moves or gestures.

Be patient, she says, can't you see we're in a dream?

In vain you'll scour the carpeted corridors and scenic panels for the sign indicating the EXIT, AUSGANG, SORTIE, USCITA.

Black, massive, compact, the silence of the vault envelops you and your descent into the lonely shadows, on the outer rim of the City of the Dead.

12

Is it the premonition of a theophany, simply a hopeful intuition, a longing for ritual purification, or the memory and brilliance of past encounters? You don't know for sure, it's probably a mixture of all that leading you to the alleyway lit by a deferential sunbeam, and on to the baths next to your local mosque. These are the critical hours of the war, with no hope of agreement or truce, when thousands of bodies incinerated by the deluge of fire lie beneath massive, black clouds, on an artificial, sulphurous night, saturated by dense fumes. Do you need to be cleansed of your moral nausea? Stripped a while of your wearisome identity? Submerged in the realm of the imprecise and opaque? You only have to cross the threshold dividing light from shadow, undress on a humble wooden bench, entrust your garments to the silent guardian of the souls in purgation at whose feet, crouching by the counter, a lean-featured youth is smoking a pipe of kef, wrapped in his threadbare djellaba and wearing an impish hat.

Are you in the subterranean Gehenna, the dwelling that exudes shadows, or the barzakh or intermediary world where, in the words of the Seal of the Saints, spirits don a subtle form? The haze blurs outlines, blinds perspectives, confers an aura of imminent danger upon the pathway across slippery floors, in between specters who tread cautiously, bloodless silhouettes, murky limbs and extremities. Will you join them, with a bucket, by the trough to the well at the world's end? Still unused to the mist, starved by the anorexic miserliness of the skylights, you'll grope your way to a spot to lie down amid the other worn-out, exhausted beings, all oneirically insubstantial. Are they also here to wash away the horror of the hetacomb, of the dry, scorching air, the dark hurricane and burning storm, the fiery, glowering craters, the carpet bombings beneath which the earth shudders and moans? Steam fuzzes their vague shapes. Some talk slowly, bent under the weight of their load, waiting for the lustral bath that is to regenerate them. Others are immobile, resting, as if lined up at the morgue, sunk in lethargy or sleep. Amid the amorphous, unclear mass, you'll make out, to your relief, the presence of a tall, well-built youth, his sturdy, robust chest and lithe, muscular limbs. A gleaming white smile sparkles on his graceful face beneath a slender black mustache. His skin seems to radiate a phosphorescent glow and, as he moves easily between sick, worn-out souls, you'll watch him cross through them without harming them, like solar light on translucent bodies. The angel—your anagnorisis was immediate—energetically and resolutely picks the buckets up, walks between the baths' customers as if they were feeble shades and heads to where you are, using the buckets to erect a kind of protected zone, destined to isolate you from everybody else, on the slabs of damp, heated marble. Didn't Ibn Arabi experience a similar apparition on his circumambulations around the Kaaba? In his to-and-froing to the well, you'll note how he modestly hides his privates behind baggy shorts and remains invisible to the rest of the assembly. You alone enjoy the sight of him and, though you are momentarily deprived of speech and can't greet him, you guess that it is Nakir himself. When the pile of buckets shields you from the eyes of others, you'll feel him sitting next to you, inviting you to lie face down. Stretched out on the freshly polished floor, you'll let him wash and knead you, inert beneath his hard, supple hands, as passive as a corpse in the act of purification. Is it time for the soul to leave and live, after its passage, the solemn moment of ritual washing? Is he going to close your eyelids, plug your ears and nostrils with cotton, tie your feet and hands over your chest, turn you towards the right, to the qibla? Nakir rubs your body ever more powerfully, pinpoints, feels tendons and muscles, submits you to stations or degrees of methodical, premeditated torture. Transformed into a mere recipient of increasingly painful, rough sensations, you won't even manage a cry of complaint when, to an accompaniment of strange wheezes, guttural sounds, and ferocious panting, he sets himself down on your tired shoulders with all his might. Quiet, as if gagged, you experience unsuspected elaborations of your torment: his brutal hands grip your shoulders, force you to double back legs and arms, tense your backbone till it bends to the rhythm of inhuman gasps! Crushed by his weight you can barely breathe. What does he want to do to you? Pull you limb from limb, paralyze you in anguished terror, mortify your guilty limbs to their breaking point? Although he keeps your face pushed against the floor blind to all sight, you will register the unimaginable scene as if your spirit had been released and could contemplate itself from the outside: like a savage bird of prey in the tremors of copulation, the angel frantically flaps his wings, sinks his claws into your back and spikes your skull with his beak! A hallucination or a real image? The pain is unbearable and to no avail you plead khalini, bel-lati, but only stoke his fury. You are at the mercy of his destructive impulse and your heart quivers in fear. What millennary crime or curse are you expiating? Is it a prelude to the interrogation of your soul and a general review of your life? Though you shout at the top of your voice, it will be too late: almost at once your thorax will be mercilessly pummeled, your ribs pulverized one by one. The angel's huffing and puffing drowns out your screams and nobody in the baths seems to notice the relentless destruction. His intense embrace fractures your brittle bones, dislocates you like a plastic doll, ruins your miserable appearance! Is he intent on tearing your extremities apart, as he lingers over his voracious feast? Only then will you bitterly realize the trap into which you have fallen. Wasn't the youth's beauty the bait your investigator used to catch you? Was the mysterious light encircling him the genuine sign of a theophany or the veil that concealed his tempting goal? How else do you explain the excruciating pressure behind, his animal cries of fitful ecstasy?

When you wake up, you will find your body restored but totally drenched in sweat.

13

And why Dante?

While recognizing his preeminent role in the establishment of his language and the haunting power of his verse, such a cold, geometrical conception of the Hereafter is surely at odds with the principles and feelings of our time? His unsparingly savage descriptions, unpalliated by the occasional note of pity, are surely incompatible with the ideals of tolerance and charity that enlighten us today?

She was sitting opposite him, the other side of the low, rectangular table, piled high with books where the small bronze mortar that usually housed his pens, erasers, pencil sharpener, and paper clips made up as usual for the missing ashtray. She was smoking, seriously smoking her Gauloises Bleues and thoughtfully had herself opened the window-catch to air the room. By tilting his head slightly to one side, he could bring back into view the panorama of roofs and garrets, chimney pots and television aerials, the bilious green dome of the Opéra and the distant, contrasting silhouettes of La Défense. Or was it just a backdrop, with the tiniest detail carefully painted in, aimed at creating the illusion that everything was as before?

Look at the color of the clouds! she exclaimed, reading

his thoughts. Don't they seem unreal?

But how could one explain the misty haze over the city, the Turks bustling behind the windows of their clothing workshops, the pigeons cooing on the grayish slate roof? She had come to return his notes on Dante and sat gazing intently at the urban vista, as if trying to establish the physical layout, perhaps to confirm she was really back. Questions crowded into his mind as he watched her there, serene, detached, perfect, unharmed by her passage on the stairs, anchored at last in accord with the *Guide* at the right level of knowledge.

Yes, but why Dante? Did his adoption of the eschatology of the earlier, cruder versions of *The Book of the Ascent* indicate any progress on man's millennary road to peace and harmony? Why the emphasis on wrath and punishment rather than forgiveness and clemency? Wasn't it better to look to the Sufis and jettison once and for all these irate maledictions?

He had got up to get the keys so he could make her a cup of coffee, but immediately abandoned the idea. How could he cross the corridor and explain his return from the shades to his wife without upsetting her and throwing her into a panic? Hadn't his weak, drip-feed loving already inflicted enough suffering without now submitting her to the test of an untimely encounter after such an irrevocable absence? He was paralyzed by the impossibility of crossing the threshold. The precarious space where he could move was clearly confined to the boundaries of his earlier room.

14

Each individual has a necessary knowledge of her own level: rushes there and can rest only there, like a child eager for the maternal breast or iron drawn to a magnet. Although you might try reaching a different one, you wouldn't succeed: you might have such a desire, but it would never be achieved. Quite the contrary; each chosen person sees the attainment of her proper level as fulfilling, as rewarding her hopes and longing.

They abandon their reading of Ibn Arabi, and follow on the screen a brief panoramic sweep of the seven heavens, the seven earths, the seven levels of hell, the circles of paradise, the various veils, lights, seas, and mountains followed by other images with a voice-over commentary:

This is the garden, planted with very tall, sturdy trees, laden with fruit, a shady resting place for all those forgiven their sins by means of purgatory. Rivers of water, milk, wine, and honey endlessly flow, limpid purification sweetening the hearts of the poets who live there: already freed of the jealousies and envies that poisoned their worldly existence, the literati now enjoy a spiritual peace that is unusual here as well as fraternal, indissoluble friendship.

If I know you, she says as she presses the stop button on her remote control, this isn't your level. I can't imagine you at one of those lively get-togethers of poets, novelists, critics, philologists, and grammarians that so delight your fellow countrymen, scoring literary points for the whole of eternity! What a cruel punishment it would be to suffer the company of academics and men-about-town, headlines-and-honors-chasers, the whole benighted throng of hangers-on, Cavafian poets, word merchants, the preening, puffed-up paper bags you flee in horror! I know full well how, despite your contempt for the literary crowd, you've maintained a vibrant friendship with a select band of authors, whose critical judgment is worth more in your eyes than any number of flattering reviews. The loss of some you hadn't seen for years because of a growing separation from worldly things has, I know, made you frustrated and nostalgic. Haven't you in fact dreamed about Jaime, a Jaime being escorted by an enervated, slinking beauty of a girl up the staircase of a Grand Hotel or palazzo, passing you by, hugging you and showing not the slightest ill-will, his features refined by the sickness that was consuming him and the complacent air of flaming youth you always reproached him for? Didn't Manuel and Reinaldo also join these nocturnal encounters till you wanted to exorcise them on the evenings of Shaaban, the gnaua ceremony of trances? And your pilgrimage to the tomb of the Poet buried in Larache, serene in spirit like a visitor to a wali, knowing full well you would come across other devotees attracted by his grace and sanctity. . . . Exceptions, naturally, to your aversion to the café-bound or televised Gatherings of Great Minds, to that bevy of domesticated fowl light years away from the souls incarnated within birds who, according to my book, fly freely through the garden of paradise, settle on branches of trees, tasting their fruits, drinking from the waters of its rivers and conversing with God!

15

What could be his proper level in the universal concert of souls?

After meandering through the clouds, frequently hindered by the horizontal or vertical flight of various angelic creatures

(angels, archangels, seraphim, cherubim, thrones, powers, dominations, according to the classification in the book of catechism you studied at school?)

to the point of endangering the subtle navigation of the souls on the waiting list, scattered like little birds over the isthmus or barzakh

(were the frantic bottlenecks the result, as she suggested, of a strike of empyrean traffic controllers, or did the excessive number of heavenly nomads grind traffic to a halt in the rush hour?)

they settled on a peak from which the planet Earth seemed like just one more ring in a coat of chain-mail, lost in the middle of a limitless, unbounded plateau.

Handsome, white-faced men and women, beautifully decked out and enveloped in a refreshing, delicate aroma, talked unhurriedly, paying no attention to the fairground booth where the Lady with the Parasol was advertising her fortune-telling powers with a flickering neon sign as a TELEVISIONARY.

They sat down on the sofa, next to a work table covered with faxes, computers, telephones. After she'd collected up all the necessary information, the Lady fed it into a huge slot machine like those in video-game arcades, fanning herself while she waited for Astroflash's reply. Then, as the contraption spewed out its answer in the form of a long trail of printed pages, she doubled them over one by one along the perforated lines till she completed the comprehensive booklet on his life. There was a long silence during which they both exchanged supportive, complicitous looks, trying to discern the nature of the sentence from the Lady's expression.

Your life is hardly exemplary, she finally said. You do agree with me, don't you?

Absentmindedly she ran her eye over the sheets without looking at anyone in particular, which she had interpreted, she whispered in his ear, as a good sign.

I know you love your wife, but her life with you hasn't exactly been a bed of roses for her, do I make myself clear? Your relationships with your sister and brothers couldn't have been more disastrous! And we'd certainly better draw a merciful veil over your writings. You yourself have confessed to being dead to decency! Oh, I know, I know: I've heard the old song-and-dance about sincerity, the let-it-all-hang-out confessions. Rubbish, ploys to catch people off guard! What do you expect me to say? Your astrological rating can't exactly be described as top-notch.

Did her words have the solid ring of truth? Half *in nebulam,* half *in latere montis,* they had withdrawn, their souls fearful and bewildered, not knowing whether he would burst into flame on Judgment Day or enter the celestial spheres, illuminated by the Highest Intelligence.

16

Probing the steamy baths, fleeing the tempting angel and his deceptive tortures, you suddenly come upon a scene of startling beauty: in a dreamy whirl, your eyes feast in turn on the vision of dozens of fierce, brawny fellows, alone or grouped together, hands clasped as if sealing a peace treaty; weight-lifters with flexed, bulging muscles; strapping, mustachioed lads, arms akimbo, lusty pectorals, radiating a glow from their leather breeches and foursquare physique. Their robust bodies, untamed features, and close-knit bonds are emblems of a vigorous faith; their musical and athletic exercises, of deeply spiritual forms of existence. When they jump up and walk round the arena where they perform, they kiss the fingertips of their right hand and skim the floor with them in a gesture of humility, pick up the boards lining the edge, and set them out by their feet, so as to encircle their leader. Facedown, legs as far apart as possible and arms open wide clinging to the ends of the boards, they execute a series of push-ups, raising their torsos, flexing their muscles, bodies undulating in an imitation of the ebb and flow of waves, the gentle ripple of marine currents. Sinuous, quivering, they seem to swim and glide on the subtle lightness of the air. Their leader encourages them by wiggling like a spirochete as he counts his helicoidal contractions and calls on Allah and the Holy Imams for their help. Only then will you spot the master's seat of honor, concealed in the shadow beyond the clusters of light converging on the arena of delights: perched in his pulpit, drum on lap, both hands beating out the exuberant rhythm, he adapts to the patterns of the chant, marks the beginning and end of each exercise, rings the bell with exquisite timing and verve. His remarkable talent stimulates, galvanizes the strength of the athletes, enraptured by hearing his epic tales, prayers to the Prophet, and delicate mystical poems. Are you dreaming, still dreaming? Are the giants armed with hefty, oblong wooden maces that they rest in the crook of their shoulders raw recruits waiting for you to give the signal to begin? When you see them simultaneously lift the maces and describe full circles around shoulder blades, ribs, and chest, is your vision real? Does the imposing appearance of the mace-bearers, transformed into heroes of a sumptuous pack of cards, reflect a material, concrete image or is it the product of an imagination dazzled by the nakedness of its uncertain, ill-defined status? Have these glorious kings of clubs with taut biceps and muscles of iron surged out of a secret, refulgent world, like beings or characters in dreams, suddenly and beautifully made flesh? Ecstasy, rapture, jubilation, joy: awareness of having reached your level, your share of immanent enjoyment and glory without your spirit even conceiving the possibility of better things! Didn't Ibn Arabi once say that, if it were not so, heaven would not be a blissful resting place but a mansion of pain and bitter disillusion? You sharpen your gaze, catch the apotheosis of the arena, that perfect ring, shape and tenor of your dual reward and punishment. Do the dervishes with the grace of slender distaffs, cutting cross-shaped silhouettes, spinning like tops or fans, possess the gift of tangibility and consistency? What fragile illusion or chimera do the athletes evoke as they tremble from head to toe, airy shrubs swaying in the breeze or the shimmering surface of a liquid stirred by a gentle breeze? When they raise their arms and their bodies flicker like pointed tongues of fire in the magic, circular space, do you still belong to the world of your body or are you experiencing a theophany, released forever from the creatures and snares of sensuousness? Drawn to the arena, illumined by the bright, intense spotlights, you admire, will forever admire the strapping lads fervently measuring the temper of their strength, each entwined in the limbs of his rival, nimbly wriggling an arm free. *Sweet as the chains of love, sings the master, are each turn and hold in the fight; / to cling to his opponent according to the rules / is pure bliss.* But you are ablaze, ablaze with them, wreathed too in their garland of flames, burning, consumed from head to foot, a creature of fire, immersed in the circle of men destined to incandescence, willing victims of their own vehemence and passion! The lack of pain takes you by surprise and, whirling in the diaphanous arena, oh divine epiphany, you will gently feel the sadness within the punishment and your own self fade and die.

17

Was there in the vision of his level a confusion of essences, a deification of humankind, an incarnation of the transcendent?

Nothing of the kind, she said. For Ibn Arabi, the multiplication of forms is the complex modulation of a single Presence. Matter, people, events, natural phenomena, works of art are its outward signs. Thus, the infinite richness and variety of the world can be resumed in scenes like the one you have described, where the body's radiant beauty is union, betrothal and rapture, proof that the self and the other are fused in one.

She put the book down on the table and burst out laughing. Her cigarette was burning away in the mortar, at a corner of the table strewn with magazines, and as soon as she noticed, she carefully stubbed it out, waving her hand in the air to get rid of the smoke.

As he could see, she'd really done her homework. The search for a quotation that appeared in a footnote to a page of her study on the Christian and Islamic eschatology in the works after Asín had become a fertile dip into an enigmatic, fascinating universe, a real ocean without shores. Did he remember the sentence from *The Crack-Up* that he'd mentioned in one of his lectures in New

York: "the test of a first-rate intelligence is the ability to hold two opposed ideas in the mind at the same time, and still retain the ability to function." That was true, wasn't it? The quotation had impressed her and she wrote it down in order to engrave it on her mind. Well, Ibn Arabi constituted the most persuasive demonstration of this seal or test. His whole work, the textual space of his work, is the site or zone in which suddenly opposites converge, antagonisms are negated, the opaque and the luminous, the obsolete and the permanent are harmoniously reconciled. Through lightning visions or instant theophanies, he leads us where he wants us to go: the whole universe, whether infidel or believer, glorifies God. Let me read you this paragraph: if we look at each other we look only at Him; if we hear each other, we hear only Him. He transfigures every face and the eye beholds Him alone. He is worshiped in everything that is worshiped. You'll think this daring, but it is how I read it: the circular arena, the goal and culmination of your desires, is a manifestation of His Presence and your entry into the circle an act of submission!

She talked hurriedly, the excitement flushing her cheeks, heightening the luminosity of her features. Through the half-opened windows (was it summertime?) they both admired, as in the old days, the washed-out gray of the roofs, the biliously green dome of the Opéra, the minute skyscrapers of La Défense, the camouflaged silhouette of Mont Valérien. The precise detail and naturalness of the conversation added to his confusion.

Wreaths of flames and tongues of fire? she asked, anticipating his objections. Forget Dante and the early versions of the Ascent! Shall we go back to the Lady with the Parasol's agency and book a guided tour of the Third Circle? Or would you rather we looked at the video of

Bosch's allegories and Doré's engravings? When the poet places his master Brunetto Latino in the circle of those convicted of the foul, abominable crime, and describes him as covered in boils, his face completely raw, how can one believe the protestations of love and respect in what is clearly just a deplorable act of revenge? Why leave him in the tormented throng, one of the horde eternally weeping over its sins with *blackened face disfigured by the fire?* What a fine example of the Christian spirit of charity! Let's return to your fellow countryman: hell is the screen that prevents man from recognizing God in all His forms, the veil covering whoever contemplates His manifestations but cannot see them. This is his crime and the reason behind his punishment!

Someone had rapped the small bronze knocker on the door to his study and they exchanged worried glances: Could people who hadn't yet entered the realm of subtlety make them out, cross their path, speak to them? They went silent, held their breath. Finally, after a tense, interminable wait, they heard the sound of something being slipped under the door followed by the squeak of footsteps hesitating on the parquet floor and the consoling hum of the elevator as it started down.

18

On the threadbare carpet in the entrance hall, a few centimeters from the door, there was a small rectangular envelope, with no indication as to the identity of either receiver or sender. He trembled as he opened it with the help of a paper knife and for her benefit read the contents out loud:

Dear Sir,

We would be most grateful if you would, as concisely as possible, give clear and detailed answers to the following questions:

1. Who are the hidden, pure, pious, faithful guardians of the mortuary in the universe, the ones who hide amongst the people to escape their gaze?
2. What was the exact date when you began to masturbate?
3. What is the number and usual consistency of your stools?

You may reply in writing although, if more convenient, the regulations equally authorize a *viva voce* statement at our offices during business hours.

Yours sincerely,
DOCTOR NAKIR AND DOCTOR MUNKAR
Expert accountants

His heart gave a turn. How had the investigators been able to locate his old hiding place in the realm of the tangible? Did they share his ease of movement in and out of both worlds?

He turned to her confused, but his confusion increased when he discovered that, although the door was still bolted and the layout of the place allowed no escape, she had quite simply vanished.

19

When he woke up or passed from one dream to another, he was disturbed by the anachronism of the situation: after her death, hadn't he left the study next to his flat where he now welcomed her in order to move himself, his books, and papers to the floor below and have direct access to his wife's apartment via a spiral staircase? If his own severing from the prison of his body had happened there, why then this imaginary or real return to the previous arrangement? Did the manifest permeability between the two worlds obey the arbitrary nature of the laws ruling dreams or was it the effect of the metamorphosing powers of the spirits that lie inactive during quarantine because of the barzakh?

20

Invest in the Hereafter! Purchase for you and your sweet spouse a building plot, a comfortable family villa, or a duplex in our luxurious apartment block with its exclusive views over the radiant celestial spheres at the different levels or circles of paradise, whatever suits your pocket! Startling reductions in specific promotional areas! Easy payment schemes, special terms for war widows and veterans!

The Lady with the Parasol is bawling through a megaphone, giving out pamphlets and brochures, displaying models of tower blocks, show flats, and building plans duly endorsed by the Town Planning and Ecology Departments.

Our holding company, from its headquarters in Tampa, Florida, in the U. S. of A., helped the experts in the High Command of the world-famous operation Desert Storm to program the extraordinary destruction/recreation of the martyred emirate, which has reactivated our tottering economy and filled the universe with admiration and awe! Now that glorious page in the history of our Stars and Stripes is turned, our Board of Directors has consulted our shareholders and decided to take the qualitative leap of extending its activities into the empyrean fields themselves, in close collaboration with the KIO and a variety of banks. Sans oublier la touche du chic et du raffinement. La différence française!

Attracted alongside other wandering shades to the projection room of the holding company, you will jointly view the promotional video, poetry courtesy of Dante, images of paradise by the grace of Doré.

Behold the holy mount of perfection and sanctuary of the soul; the intelligence of the spheres reflecting the rays from on high, making their mark on matter! The terrace from which you have enjoyed these views belongs, as you can see, to a family duplex in our model apartment block, equipped with every comfort you might aspire to as your just reward for a life devoted to business and the triumph of our ideals of progress and justice. Take a look at the detail in the living room, the panoramic lounge, telescopes adjusted to capture both the flight of heavenly creatures and the path of our ballistic missiles! The conquests of technological progress all ready to serve your eternal enjoyment and personal well-being! And everything at unbeatable prices, all within reach of your pocket!

Then suddenly

Merde! Mais qu'est-ce que c'est ça?

Instead of shots of the sublunary world and blissful visions, the screen replicates images of devastation and ruin, a traffic jam of blazing vehicles, lethal fumigations from planes skimming the ground, carbonized bodies, helicopters vomiting flames, scenes of panic, ants scattering frantically, human torches, the gasping faces of women and children, deprived of oxygen, fire, more fire, apocalypse, horror, one vast collective cremation.

(Voice-over: Say hello to Allah!)

Someone (genie or genius?) has switched the video tape in the recorder that's plugged into our Lady of the Parasol's television set!

21

Was it a memory he had exhumed of his spiritual exercises in the Order's house in Manresa or a later reworking in the light of what Blanco White wrote in his *Autobiography* and the evocations of Stephen Dedalus as outlined by Joyce? The terrifying depiction of the torments, the simile of the little bird and the grain of sand removed by its beak from the vast beach every ten thousand years, the hapless story of the adolescent hurled into the eternal flames because of a solitary sinful act, and all recounted with theatrical guile and hollow mimicry to a silent audience terrorized after several days of hermetic isolation corresponded, she said, to a miserable, third-rate version of the popular eschatology of ignorant preachers and fear-mongerers. Nobody these days believed in fire and brimstone or in the tale of the child who, because of a single bad thought, is still bubbling away in one of Old Nick's cauldrons, after being knocked down by a righteous bus!

They had settled down in a meadow near the garden of good fortune and could survey the well of the waters of ecstasy whose contents transmute into the flame of living love, the spring that reflects the allegorical Eyes of the Beloved, the tree that grows within the contemplative soul, the spirits of the innocents incarnated in the swift-flighted birds with brilliant white plumage. As he didn't believe his senses, she was quick to reassure him. It all appeared in Sufi poetry and the Lady with the Parasol would not disturb that tranquillity with her inopportune prattle!

She had carefully read the background material related to the text and, although she couldn't help him in his work or translate his papers, her accumulated experience of the barzakh allowed her to enlighten him and corroborate the illuminations and epiphanies of the Seal of the Saints. Gehenna exists, she said, but the eternity of one's stay there does not imply everlasting torment. Mercy is extended to all beings and the reprobates' fire will be transformed into a refreshing peace. If creatures of land, air, and water can exist, why not creatures of fire? Isn't fire perhaps the most beautiful and active of the four elements? The beings who burn, whatever the gravity of their guilt, live in accord with the law of their nature and would suffer if deprived of what that requires, as fish asphyxiate when taken out of water. For fire is their habitat and it is there that they will know eternal happiness. What a genial way to interpret the revealed text! Can you imagine the scandalized theologians and keepers of the canon? Look at the circle of athletes, radiating bliss! Mustaches twirling over handsome faces, lean muscles, compact bodies, "like a prismatic block of crystal, pure, self-sufficient majesty"! How often have you thrown yourself on your knees enthralled by their prodigious forms, the splendor of their attributes, their solid, mineral density? Blind to the theophany of a universe where even the stones glorify Him, you worshiped them like idols. The proliferation of things and beings distracted you. Now, in a state of peaceful recollection, you can capture the harmonious concert of the elements with a pure, serene mind. Take another look at the video of the arena and the ceremonial men of brawn! You will burn with them, alongside the sturdiest, the most leonine, your bodies licked by the flames till coupled, fused into one. Wasn't this what you were vaguely searching for when you decided to write the book?

22

His wife! How could that possibly be?

Had she temporarily abandoned the realm of the sensuous in order to greet him or was he the one who had taken a step backwards, breaking and entering a world that was dead and gone? The intimate, apparently normal space of his home was as disturbing as those moments of illusory calm that come before the explosion of a torrential storm. While he furtively removed his warm outer garments, he heard her walking in the kitchen, taking the ice cubes out of the refrigerator. He tiptoed towards the living room, fearful a sudden gesture might break the fragile balance of the elements. Opposing ideas and feelings clashed in his innermost self. Should he greet her tenderly, tearfully, as the exceptional circumstances demanded? Rush into her arms, give free rein to the emotion that was overpowering him? What rational, plausible explanation could there be for his disappearance and return? Didn't he run the risk of shocking her, perhaps of depriving her of the use of her senses? Nevertheless, as he went in, he had heard her call his name from the kitchen quite naturally! It was glass-of-whiskey time, after a day probably working or visiting friends. The place seemed plagued with traps, and after considering various options—rushing to see her in the kitchen, making himself scarce via the inside staircase to his study, feigning a call of nature and taking refuge in the bathroom while waiting on developments—he decided to stay in the small sitting room and sink down into his armchair with an air of apparent calm.

Has your work gone well? she asked as she finally emerged in her burgundy caftan and sat down on the sofa after setting the ice bucket on the floor.

He swallowed, unable to manage more than a hmm, excited, confused as to his own state and the reality of the scene.

Why hadn't she been surprised by his arrival or simply brushed her lips against his as she usually did after one of his absences? It was as if he'd just been for a walk in the neighborhood or hadn't even left the flat! He waited a few moments, hiding his face in the evening newspaper and pretending to be entranced by news of the war. The number of the coalition's airborne missions had reached the fantastic figure of seventy thousand take-offs! The dispatches from the special correspondents emphasized the high level of preparedness of officers and command for the imminent land offensive!

I took your phone messages, she interjected. Nothing important; a bookseller left his number. By the way, when I went down to your room, I found an annotated copy of *The Divine Comedy* on the step. How did it get there? Was it dropped accidentally? She was quite matter-of-fact, totally oblivious to the unusual nature of this encounter, too involved in the daily routine to take note of his trembling hands and deep embarrassment. Her calm expression and occasional smiles clearly revealed the absence of anxiety or reproaches. It was almost as if, when he was eclipsed from the ephemeral world, his double had stayed by her side functioning as a husband should. Which of the two was real? The one who wandered through the mists of the barzakh or the one who had stayed in the flat?

He took advantage of a call for his wife—My father, she sighed—to get out of the armchair, glance at the layout of the room and check that nothing had changed, to go down the inside staircase and take a quick look at his work area. The room light was on and the first thing he saw was her photo—fair-haired, clear blue eyes, a gold chain round her neck—that he had put on the sideboard on his return to the city just over a year ago, after her exodus to the realm of subtlety while he was on his travels. His eyes quickly ran over the bookshelves next to his desk: dictionaries, commentaries, reference works, everything still in place. Scattered over the table, he found a few uncorrected sheets of his manuscript. He picked one of them up and discovered, to his confusion, that they corresponded to the draft of the present chapter.

23

He dreamt he had written a story by Ibn Arabi.

"If you were to ask me, 'Well, what is Shauhari's story?' I could tell you how, as he himself recounts, he left home one fine day in a state of ritual impurity to take yeasted flour to the baker's. After leaving it in the shop, he went to the banks of the Nile to comply with his ablutions and, while in the river, he saw himself, the way we see ourselves in dreams, as if he were in Baghdad. He'd married, been living with his wife for six years and had had several children by her, I can't remember how many. Then he came to, still in the water, finished purifying himself, got out of the river, dressed, went to the baker's to pick up his bread, and returned home to tell his family everything revealed to him in that vision. After several months had gone by, the woman from Baghdad whom he had seen himself married to in the Nile came to his city and found out his address. When she reached his house he immediately recognized both her and the children, and could not deny they were his. He asked her when she had married and she said: 'Six years ago, and these are our children.' And so what had happened in the imagination took on a concrete form in the sensuous world. This is one of the six things mentioned by Dhu'l Nun al Misri which ordinary minds judge to be impossible."

Was what happened a literary manifestation of the pleasure of unlikely imaginings as defended by Blanco White and experienced by Borges? Or, as his wife observed when he showed her the text, merely Shauhari's cunning ruse to justify outright bigamy, by disguising it beneath a halo of sanctity for the benefit of his family. What he could be sure of was that if *she* had been the Egyptian wife, she wouldn't have swallowed the tale or welcomed the wife from Baghdad and her horde of children!

Fortunately, she lovingly added before abandoning the dream and vanishing, at least she didn't run that kind of risk with him!

24

The beast has already got her paws over the threshold and staked her claim on the doorway, and though I want to stop her coming in, my efforts shatter against her sovereign indifference as, with a cold majestic air, she leisurely takes over the place, paces proprietorially through the house, stretches out on the carpet at the foot of my bed, and gazes at me for hours on end. I can't make out her shape clearly, only those pupils staring at me. By my side night and day, impassively she haunts my every step or move, completely untouched by the busy flow of visitors. Neither my mother, father, nor my stepfather, not even the doctor summoned by the family seem to become aware of that presence. They walk past without seeing her, take my pulse, ask after my health and appetite, voice worries about my mental state. When I mention her, they don't listen, but shower encouraging words upon me, divert the conversation along other paths. They talk of temporary alienation, split personality. They are unable to perceive the shining, green, asymmetrical eyes, sometimes encrusted like emeralds on the blurred contours of her head, sometimes hanging in midair, afloat, parallel, unfathomable eyes alert to my slightest gesture. Spying on me, ever restless, eyes locked on mine, yet always multiplying, in motion: from door and carpet, from window and ceiling. Already there are several pairs, set in different parts of the room, in the psychiatric hospital they move me to: always green, shining, asymmetrical, perfectly compact and opposed, trained on me wherever I look, even if I keep my eyes closed. What I've feared ever since childhood, from the moment my father died, is a reality. The beast with the prying eyes has burst in upon my life, taken possession of my soul and senses, rules my mind, governs my will. Its inquisitive eyes are everywhere, proliferating like a malignant virus, peppering me from all sides: I find them between the folds of my sheets, served up on the breakfast tray, immersed in the glass of water with the pills my doctor has prescribed. Why can't they see them? Are they so obtuse and blind they can't see them? To escape these people, I sneak out of the hospital, give the security guards the slip, run to the station in that hateful neighborhood with its neat lines of houses, surgically clean streets, and little posters warning of dogs as merciless and savage as their owners, I catch the train to Paris, get off on the platform at the Gare du Nord. Years later, when I read your book and came across the enigmatic phrase you use to describe me—"the piercing scream of the girl staggering across the station lobby creates around her a sacred space inaccessible to the curious bystanders outside her delirium" —I freed myself from space and time, and saw myself back in the huge lobby swarming with people, pursued by the beast's infinitely multiplying eyes, cutting my path through the people summoned then dispersed by the loudspeakers, concentrating all my helplessness and terror into the uttering of that cry. Although you don't designate me, I knew I was the one designated there. It's unimportant whether you'd witnessed the scene or not—around that time wasn't the Gare du Nord your pickup point on your ascent through the dwelling places of the soul?—the eye of imagination had discovered me. I think the premonition of our encounter saved my life and allowed me to survive those solitary times. My escape hadn't been in vain and I returned to hospital. Gradually, the eyes of the beast weakened their grip, curbed their assault, lifted their siege, slowly dissolving in the aseptic atmosphere of that house of lunatics where my family had sent me. Although I couldn't be certain, I sensed someone had caught the meaning of my cry and discovered their own invulnerability in its defiance of logic. From then on I felt an inner voice calling me, a soft whistle coming from my most secret self that left me in suspense, seeing it so close and yet so distant, for however much I struggled, I could never get a hold on it. But I felt I was cured, able to face existence, move away from my family, try my fortune in America, marry, separate, follow my studies at the university till the day I met you by chance at an absurd dinner for professors and graduates on Morningside Drive when I was convinced, even before I read your book, that you'd helped me through my worst moment of helplessness and tribulation. Finally hiding away, after my passage and journey to the barzakh, I was relieved to discover you weren't in the cemetery with everyone else. My spirit was already enjoying its transparency and images from the world were being etched there, independent of time or place. Listen carefully: elaborate your text by taking advantage of my direct experience of the intuitions of the novelists and mystics to whom you introduced me. Can you see how dreams, which only the eye of the imagination perceives, penetrate what has happened, what happens, what will happen, before anything happens? Which faculty, apart from our imagination, possesses the gift of spanning moments of space and time, shuffling them together and condensing the universe, the whole universe into the privileged cast of a book?

25

It's not the Lady with the Parasol's video or a slide show of Gustave Doré's illustrations. The urban space you're wandering through offers an endless succession of ruins, bomb craters, facades in precarious equilibrium, truncated minarets, carbonized remains of buses, tanks abandoned with their crews, service stations in flames, houses with gaping sockets and black yawning holes, remnants of the pillaging and orgy of blood, victims of summary executions enveloped in unbreathable air, sweet stench of decomposing bodies, crowds of civilians blasted in full retreat, wide-eyed with panic, bullet-riddled foreheads, contorted hands pointing an accusing finger at the invisible author of the butchery. Sacrificed like guinea pigs on the altar to new military technology or to the crazed loser's need for vengeance? The vague angle of your vision prevents you from giving a precise answer to the question. You don't know where you are or how you could have got there, and reached the spot before the jackals and the enemy's advance guard. Are the reprobates Dante ignored Kurds, Shi'ites, Palestinians, panic-stricken deserters, or simply children of fertile Mesopotamia clinging to the last to their instinct for life, the only solid truth that is beyond dispute? Have you perhaps reached the first floor of Gehenna, that plain or prison of the winds whose inhabitants, according to travelers, eat their own flesh and drink their own blood? The ground is littered with random objects abandoned in the exodus of a wandering people history has cruelly hidden from the light of justice: saucepans, eiderdowns, blankets, old-fashioned garments, gas stoves, a doorless refrigerator, children's shoes, odd boots, soldiers' caps, a bald, mutilated doll, a sheep chewing make-believe grass roped up to its owner's stiff, garrotted hand. A magnetic attraction more powerful than your horror forces you to halt and examine one by one the bodies that have fallen on the pavements, street corners, sewers, and crossroads of the phantom city, flattened by bombing raids and finished off by the tyrant: a young boy, face corroded by phosphorus, his halfmelted eyelids hanging down in a fringe; two soldiers incinerated by a laserguided weapon, recognizable only by their cartridges and useless helmets; the body of a corpse without extremities, clothed only in flies. A still-confused if stubborn presentiment alerts you, prevents you from lingering there. Is it trying to spare you the painful descent to the lower reaches of the underworld, where a river of boiling sulphur courses, inmates stare eyeless, and huge serpents devour sinners? The anguish overtaking you and lodging in your innermost self suggests the imminence of more painful, closer-to-home images, the exhuming of deeper wounds that will never heal. You walk on hesitatingly, despite the haze and stench of bodies, towards the fallen, prostrate figure of a well-dressed woman, wrapped in an elegant fox fur and wearing a fashionable thirties hat. The rays of a luminous aura reach out diffusely, tenuously, as they abandon her body, isolating her from her surroundings and seeming to send out a message aimed expressly at you. The premonition galvanizes your energies, puts warnings and advice to one side, ominously, incredulously, takes root in your mind. Who is she? What's she doing here? Why don't you dare turn her over and look her in the face? Are you afraid you won't recognize her after so long despite the photographs of her that you've kept? Or that she'll dazzle you with the beauty and fullness of her face, made from a living flame? You hold your breath, bend down to the bag she's holding tightly and confirm, beyond dread, the chilling precision of memory; all your presents are intact. Is she the mother of flesh-and-blood beings with ligaments, nerves, bone and marrow, or the symbol and incarnation of all mothers who have been equally caught out shopping when the bombs dropped on Barcelona, Basra, or Baghdad? Hasn't the lapse of a lifetime exorcised her specter? Which spark fed the nightmare and restored to the rawness of the vision what should have remained buried in the depths of the subsoil?

26

You close your eyes and, warming to the silence and tranquillity, skim lightly almost at ground level, over streets, pantheons, mausoleums, clusters of graves where you ranged years ago, corseted in your body, on a slowly fertile, entrancing stay that you cannot and will not ever forget. Wrapped in a threadbare blanket, between the monument to someone deceased half a century ago and the old man's pallet, it was there you experienced your first inner ecstasy and imagined visit to the kingdom of shades, freed by sleep from material form, and fleetingly united with the pleiad of wandering souls who people Al Kharafa and vanish into sepulchers and secret vaults at the break of day. Master of your subtle state, you now glide swiftly, effortlessly, over solitary Sufi lodges, striated domes, slender minarets, exhuming images and memories of your daytime promenade: dusty streets, crumbling facades, stunted little trees, rubbish, rustic looms, private oratories, dovecotes, gardens, residential districts. The white moonlight bathes green- and ocher-painted houses, patios decorated with flowers and mosaic Koranic verse, bowls of water and palm fronds left on the graves. The fragile sounds of life in the medina have faded away with the last light bulbs, candles, and gas lamps. Families, flocks, domestic fowl have gone back to their households and are enjoying the peace and cool of night after the punishing sun, the dusty oppression of day. It is the vibrant moment of sleep, when those buried in the mausoleums leave their sepulchers and communicate with the sleeping through the wakeful imagination. The pillars of society pictured in frock coats and red fezes in the photographs hanging from the cenotaphs check the guards are resting, peer cautiously out at the deserted patios, melancholy witnesses to the spectacle of their own inevitable ruin and decay. Do you fly on the wings of Israfil, huge like the wings of the cockerel in the first heaven, whose head, according to the chroniclers of the Ascent, reaches the lower reaches of God's Throne? Or do you enjoy the delight of hovering lightly, an exhilarating sense of danger, the rapture of weightlessness? No soul now hangs on the news bulletins from the clean war, the actions of intelligent weapons on deadly surgical missions, but the impact of a diffuse distress disturbs the resting inhabitants with visions of death and desolation, landscapes covered in ash and flakes of fire. Is that the anguish that troubles Ahmed's sleep, gasping in his wife's arms, oblivious to your furtive presence after such a long absence? Creeping away from that intimate scene, you think you can hear the voice of a Koranic reader chanting sura 67 at one of the street stalls set up by families of the deceased to commemorate the quarantine. The devout souls of Rabiaa and Al Bisthami sweep down in a flurry from the almost vertical escarpment of the Mountain and the spires and domes of the Citadel. Are you also dreaming or, purged and stripped bare, do you enjoy blissful beatitude? Thanks to imagination, have you transcended the limits of time and space, are you mingling the living and the suggested, levitating but keeping your feet on the ground? For you can see Al Bistami's funeral at the moment the cortege escorted by a cloud of green birds hears the muezzin's call, and as he proclaims the Uniqueness of God, the corpse waves a hand under the shroud and points skyward, just as the translucent shades surrounding the grave of the Beloved of Pure Love run their fingertips over each corner, raise them delicately to their faces, kneel next to the sepulcher, caress its mantle, half chant, half moan their prayers. Do the anachronisms, the charisma, the collision of levels correspond to the faculties of the deceased in quarantine or extend to the whole gathering of shades? The beauty and peace of the macabre, its railings, iron gates, balustrades, funeral stelas, hovels with their pilgrim drawings of the Kaaba, handprints in sacrificial lambs' blood on the walls, send you into a rapturous swoon. She has returned to your side and, while she points to your own body asleep in Paris during the transhumance just described, she will murmur, flourishing her hand over the creatures and objects present in your text, blind is the eye that does not see you watching over it.

27

The small lounge, its plush armchairs arranged in a semicircle around the television set, has been gradually filling up with people, regulars from the hotel bar or tourists who've lost their way, as the time draws near for the next news bulletin on the ceasefire and imminent end to hostilities.

You are among strangers, deprived both of her comforting immediacy and of the celestial nomads who ordinarily encircle you. The publicity slots monotonously follow each other and, finally, after the signature tune and images that introduce the program you've been waiting for, the Lady with the Parasol appears on the screen, wearing her lilac organdy dress, lace flounces and big bows, necklaced with glass beads, medallions and cameos, with white stockings, high-heeled shoes, a spangled, imitation diamond buckle on the instep. After issuing greetings to her right and to her left, she sits down at the triangular head of a microphone-strewn table and welcomes her guest stars for the evening, celebrities from intellectual and literary life, summoned to view the news transmitted live by satellite and to follow up the events with their comments

—a philosopher with long wavy locks who's the spitting image of George Sand

—a psychoanalyst author of numerous works that make him an authority in the field

—a politicologist, ex-Kremlinologist, opportunely recycled into Islamology

and, surprise, surprise!

—the lean-featured youth, wrapped in a threadbare djellaba, wearing an impish hat, who was smoking a pipe of kef crouched down in the entrance to the baths.

After several sequences of cleancut military smiles, explanatory graphics with moving arrows and targets lit up by flashing lights, gentle images of ballistic missiles destroying remote, impersonal targets, the Lady with the Parasol turns to her guests and invites them to have their say.

GEORGE SAND: There's no such thing as a beautiful war, but there are just wars, and these people asked for it by being so pig-ignorant! Their primeval herd instinct and love of tyranny put them beyond the pale of historical progress, like a residual, unpredictable, amorphous magma.

THE PSYCHOANALYST: Their identity is rooted in an umbilical fantasy structuring a wholly symbolic source, which is all the more active for being unconscious. The dream of a common Matreya—mother, language, religion, land—that is homogeneous and pure, with no interference from the Other, in the last analysis presupposes the nonexistence of the father and the sublimation of incest.

THE POLITICOLOGIST: And when is it ever going to end! Who can guarantee that later on another self-proclaimed genius won't devote his oil or other revenues to tinkering around with chemical, biological, or nuclear warfare, before he invades his neighbors and threatens the West with terrorism and, given the wherewithal, widescale destruction? However improbable this may seem at present, in the long term it is by no means an idle hypothesis!

THE YOUTH IN THE DJELLABA AND IMPISH HAT:

يا عباد الله، خبثوني

Shock, clearing of throats, shouts of protest, insults: The fucking nerve of that punk! What the hell's he talking about? Can't anyone here translate his gibberish? Why didn't they send us someone more presentable? Or are all his compatriots a bunch of animals?

George Sand, the psychoanalyst, and the politicologist elaborate new and brilliant theories about Oedipus complexes, immaturity, fossilization, the narcissistic paranoia befuddling the minds of the hypnotized masses, but nobody is listening: the enraged audience prefers action to words and is pelting rotten eggs and tomatoes at the dirty A-rab in the djellaba!

The Lady with the Parasol takes an amber cigarette holder from her bag, inserts a Philippine cigarette, lights up with her Ronson, and exhales a cloud of smoke to calm herself amid the general mayhem. She has apparently left the screen, since she walks over and plants herself in front of you with all the fury of her outraged dignity.

Congratulations! she barks. Aren't you ashamed at distancing yourself from this beautiful moral consensus that is nothing less than the foundation of a new world order?

28

Isn't the process of novelistic creation a quarantine? Shouldn't the author, during the spell he needs to compose his work, withdraw from the world and establish a veritable cordon sanitaire around himself and his raw materials, which is properly secured and defended? Doesn't the contagious power of writing, of which he is first its victim before he becomes its vehicle, require the seclusion imposed on a colony of lepers or on monks possessed by God in their enclosed order? That rash venture of assembling and ordering the elements of a text in a vague, imprecise zone, establishing a fine web of relationships, weaving a net of meanings beyond time and space, ignoring the laws of verisimilitude, rejecting worn-out notions of character and plot, abolishing the frontiers between reality and dream, destabilizing the reader by multiplying the levels of interpretation and registers of voice, appropriating historical events and using them to fuel his purpose, living, dying, resurrecting for himself and everybody else, must surely require all that be concentrated in a mental space specially prepared to incubate the contaminating sickness and prevent it spreading before its time? Like other epidemics, the one that germinates in the creative field of the novelist seeks, after the quarantine is over, to extend itself naturally into the reader's receptive mind, the objective of its fruitful, infectious project. From the minute the latter engages in the risky adventure, he finds himself in quarantine, isolated from the world in a bubble of his own, absorbed in the pleasures of his contagion. Quarantine for the author, quarantine for the reader, quarantine for the book, vital to the active, transforming power of the written word! Indeed, hasn't the eye of the imagination been secularized in the field of eschatology by the novelists who excite his own admiration?

29

His wife had advised him to take the bus—the 93 from the Porte Saint-Martin will drop you right on the corner, she'd said—but his deep-rooted hankering for the métro won out and, ignoring the inconvenience of changing stations and trains, he plunged down the nearest entrance and into the subsoil of the city, delighted to discover that the automatic gate and barrier opened before him without need of a ticket, as if moved by supernatural respect. That seemed to auger well and, while traveling in a crowded compartment, he held his briefcase close to his chest with the books and documents destined to vouchsafe his sincerity and good faith when questioned by his investigators. The three typed questions didn't present too many difficulties, but hours after receiving the mysterious missive, he found a fourth, written in invisible ink on the back of the sheet of paper, the meaning of which perplexed him as it became transparent: "What kind of book are you writing and what role do we play in it?" That was impossible to clarify in writing and he had decided to avail himself of the possibility, as indicated in the regulations, of making a spoken statement on the issue at the office of the Accounts Tribunal. In order not to lose heart and to preserve the necessary sangfroid, he concluded that yet again it was Munkar trepanning with the intention of putting his nerves to the test and gauging his mental agility and natural irony. As he had explained to her after the passage, his brief experience of him roundly belied the tales of his severity and so-called outbursts of sadism.

(As for his partner, things weren't so clear!)

The Tribunal was round the corner from the station and he went off in that direction fancy free, clinging as always to his briefcase of evidence and documentation, fears allayed by the normality of the place and the calm on the faces of the people also heading there for one reason or another. He went up the front steps, not allowing himself to be overawed by the threatening majesty of the columns of the facade, entered the huge hallway thronged by members of the public, waited his turn in the line at the information counter, and was given a card indicating the floor, corridor, and office number of his examiners; a differently colored card carried his own identification number. A bushy-browed flunky with a goatee led him affably from the noisiest, most crowded areas to higher and apparently empty floors where silence reigned. He pointed to a bench at one end of the corridor and asked him to wait there. When they're ready, they'll tell you, he added. He mumbled his thanks and sat down, briefcase on lap, using the interlude to memorize his replies so they would come out naturally. The waiting didn't worry him: he knew his examiners lacked resources and couldn't finish business quickly however much they strived. Every so often, a door on the corridor opened and a woman's head emerged fleetingly to ascertain his presence, enough time to give him a neutral once-over and disappear. As the waiting was prolonged, he got up, stretched his legs, and took a stroll. The corridor was still deserted, but behind the massive oak office doors he could discern the hustle and bustle of functionaries, telephone calls, and the tap-tap of typewriters. Other doors filtered the muffled sound of questions formulated through loudspeakers, intercut by much groaning and moaning. Making sure nobody was spying on him, he stopped in front of a door embellished with a print of naked men and women, with dogs' mouths, goats' ears, bulls' hooves and sheep's wool: though muted, cries and laments reached him, gusts from an ill wind. In the adjacent office, a polyglot notice forewarned him that there they had registered and archived, as in the Customs, the totality of the sins of the tormented soul where *ice locks in Cocytus.* If his memory didn't deceive him, didn't that line come from canto 31 of the *Inferno?* When he was about to push the door ajar and take a peek inside, the sliding of a bolt made him draw back and quickly return to the bench signaled by the flunky. He was confronted by a bespectacled, bad-tempered woman. Your number, she said. He handed the card to her and immediately opened his briefcase to show her his medical certificate and the results of his tests. As you can see, the frequency and texture of defecations are absolutely normal, with no irregularities or evidence of parasites. Nor is there any sign of the presence of albumen, which betokens a cancerous inflammation of the intestinal mucosa. He cleared his throat: as for the previous question, if you will allow me to reverse the order, after digging deep in my memory, thinking back to summers at the family holiday home, I think I can state that I first masturbated at the age of twelve, that is, in 1943, probably in the month of July. . . . But the impatient, disagreeable look on the functionary's face led him to cut short his explanations: I think Drs. Nakir and

Munkar would rather receive my statement in person.

Suddenly all the doors along the corridor opened and dozens of identical heads appeared gradually shrinking into the distance, as in a fairground hall of mirrors,

(or a scene from *The Lady from Shanghai,* your wife butts in, who has come in the room to say hello without your noticing and is reading the last paragraph over your shoulder)

analyzing you from head to toe with their accusingly suspicious, penetrating eyes.

Who told you Nakir and Munkar work here? bellows the female functionary. Despite the excessive numbers of emigrants we have the misfortune to take in, their jurisdiction has never spilled over our frontiers! Your personal data in any case isn't coming up on our computer screens and we can't take any responsibility for your file even if you are a hundred percent Apostolic, Roman, and Catholic. Better catch a direct flight to Cairo. At their airport they'll find you a pen-pusher to sort through the red tape. Get yourself a taxi and go to the southern macabre: they'll be there at night in one of the mausoleums or Sufi lodges in the City of the Dead.

30

The moral quarantine of the war had cut into his life, its bloody images and oneiric visions persistently warding off sleep and undermining the flow of his day. The unusual silence in the medina of the Seven Holy Men had deepened as days went by and awareness of the magnitude of the disaster took root in the minds of the inhabitants he bumped into on his sporadic visits to the Square. The occasional stroll to that once luminous stage nourished rays of hope for continuity of life, sorely shaken and tried by the diffuse aggression it suffered.

There was a time when his attention centered on Saruh: youth had yet to scorn him, leaving him troubled and tetchy and, drawn by the compass of desire, he sought him out, was tugged towards him as he meandered. His eloquence, humor, and furtive complicity beyond the daily display in the halqa consummated his notion of happiness. Firmly anchored in the Square, the center of his delights, he admired the arrogance of his stance, his shaven skull, powerful neck, gold-capped teeth, silvery tongue, visible strength, his guardsman ruggedness. Everything had receded far into the distance, thrown off course by the lightness of time, that swift, elusive deer.

Now he only came upon shades that arose with him from the darkness, grim, intense faces, the faithful awaiting the muezzin's call, traders sitting by the door to their deserted bazaars, the ears of young and old glued to radios. The tourists had disappeared from the souks: the panoramic terraces of the Glacier and the Hôtel de France were completely empty.

As intently as a man condemned to death, he gazed at the tight rumps of the dazzling snow-covered mountains that peered over the top of the pink and ocher buildings, clearly outlined against the pure blue sky. He had nodded towards the gnaua masters sitting in the café and sought out the consoling immediacy of Cherkaui, the last Sufi of the halqa. He found him at his usual stall, with his mat, tame pigeons, snake-skins threaded with hermit shells, his ragged, patched djellaba, hirsute, disheveled face, a prickly sight suffused with secret sweetness. Silently he sat down next to him, attentive to his chanting prayers and passionate incantations to love and charity. Trapped between the logic of war and the logic of money, was it possible the primordial words could survive, however fragilely? The old man had recognized him and broke off his litany to kiss him. A feeling of peace and friendship raced through his body, like an analgesic after a sharp, stabbing pain. Cherkaui's benign serenity seemed to spread through the halqa, endowing the circle of spectators with a delicate moral beauty.

When he spotted her, almost translucent, in the middle of the ring, he felt no surprise: only happiness at meeting her again in a city she never knew and which she would undoubtedly have fallen in love with. She was wearing an ordinary T-shirt and jeans and stood there calmly, as if she were waiting for him outside the lecture room, enthralled by her reading of Quevedo, among amateur musicians, hippies, students, black Puerto Rican basketball players, on the sunny lawn in Washington Square next to the university.

31

They were in their living room commenting on the latest vicissitudes in the war—subdued by the unusual silence in the city which, from the first flash, seemed to have sunk of its own accord into a curfew of fear—when the telephone suddenly resounded. His wife picked up the receiver and jammed it to her ear. It must be a call from abroad, she said: it's a very strange sound. Mechanically he picked up his annotated copy of Dante and began rereading for the nth time the description of the ninth circle of hell, trying to discover, without too much conviction, new parallels with those of al-Saqar and al-Tara, the lair and mansion of Satan and his armies according to the early versions of the *Miradj.* Yes, he's here, his wife said after a while. Who's that? Sorry? She passed him the phone, trying to cover the receiver with her hand: it's the office of Messrs Natir and Munar, I couldn't hear very clearly; at any rate from Egypt. His heart gave a turn: he needed a few moments to regain his composure and cleared his throat before deciding to speak: hello? One moment, rasped a feminine, slightly bullying voice, please don't hang up! An interminable wait began, accompanied by piercing sounds, squeaks, snatches of conversation in Arabic and English. The voice repeated at intervals, don't hang up, we're tracing your call, and then the line went dead. He waited, held his breath, and gradually, as the suspense was prolonged, he thought he heard angry gusts of wind, pleading voices, human groans, a muffled explosion of engines. He noticed that while the operator's words became more distant, more spaced out, the noises and shouting were getting louder, acquiring a threatening nearness. Great tongues of flame poured down and the sand caught light like tinder! Was it the operator expressing herself in these terms or had he been mistakenly connected to the blast furnace and hoist of a steelworks or the demolition site of a bunker apocalyptically pounded by cranes? Hello there! he shouted. But he only heard the rhythmic throbbing of drills or steam hammers crushing rubbish. Were the howls reaching his ears from defenseless bodies buried under the dust and savage clamor of the machines? The obviously recorded message was lost in a shattering confusion of wails, pleas, and laments. What should he do? Put the phone down? Insult his investigators' sense of hierarchy and dignity by setting them against him? Might they not be deliberately submitting him to that test to measure his patience and the respect owed to their authority? A violent, stentorian burst of laughter, magnified, echoing round a huge cavern or vault dispelled any doubts. Who but they could laugh like that? The certainty he had them at the end of the line infused him with inner gentleness. He was cheerfully wondering which of the two he should talk to first when he was abruptly cut off. Crestfallen, he waited for a few moments before shouting at the top of his voice: are you there, Madam? The line's been cut. Madam, can you hear me? But he could only hear an answering machine repeating endlessly in Arabic: Because the lines are congested we cannot deal with your call. Please try again in a few moments!

32

He imagined how, by turning away from the straight path where he had slipped off his sandals before acceding to the luminous spheres described by Ibn Arabi, he entered upon a landscape of uncultivated, low-lying scrubland, known in his language as a wilderness. He saw to his right, in the area of the first heaven, a singing angel whose top half was snow and bottom half fire, inviting all creatures subtle and gross to fuse the charity in their hearts in a single body, as his own combined snow and fire despite their natural opposition. Gloomily he counted the rare travelers ever more distant on the straight road, making their way to the light: someone offered bowls of honey, wine, and milk to slake their thirst and, following the Prophet's example, they deliberately chose milky perfection. But his own difficult path, tortuous and uneven across barbed wire and artificial darkness, forced him to advance very tentatively, afraid of falling and being sucked down one of the pits at the side of the road, crawling with serpents and vermin. She had followed the band of pilgrims to the light and signaled to him to go back. Unhappily, as in the vision of the walkers of Salé that befell Ibn Arabi, his feet wouldn't obey him. Then he spotted the Lady with the Parasol, wearing a dress of lilac organdy, lace flounces and big bows, necklaced with glass beads, medallions and cameos, with white stockings, high-heeled shoes, a spangled, imitation diamond buckle on the instep. She was smoking a cigarette in a holder, and frantically fanning herself, as if stifled by the heat.

Bonjour l'ami, ne soyez pas si pressé! la route est très longue et fatigante. Vous ne voulez pas boire un verre avec moi?

(She's back again? Hadn't he left her with the panel of Islamologists in the television studios?)

Hep jeune homme! Si je me permets de vous appeler come ça en dépit du fait que vous n'ayez plus vingt ans c'est parce que vous conservez le charme et l'esprit de la jeunesse, sa séduction! J'aimerais pouvoir parler avec vous dans un endroit plus intime. . . .

Her blue saucer eyes, encircled by false eyelashes and crows' feet, matched her gluttonous, greedy mouth, the tip of her sinuous tongue, a pouting, saucy little number suddenly overtaken by her years.

Je connais un motel près d'ici. Chambres tout confort, boissons, lumière indirecte, matelas aquatique, vidéos porno. . . .

She winked at him, like the shutter of a camera between takes.

Venez, je vous prends par le bras! Il n'y a rien de meilleur au monde qu'une bonne partie de jambes en l'air avec une experte comme moi!

(Was the Grand Guignol shot of her face going to go on and on? He pushed her away and at that very instant woke up.)

33

You were in your Paris house, in bed with your wife, absorbed in the book you intended to write and, after you'd dozed off, a tall, handsome youth appeared before you, all strong, sturdy chest, and slender, sinewy limbs. His skin glowed softly phosphorescent and, because of his subtlety and lightness, you realized he was the very same incarnation from the baths. Arise, dress, and follow me, he said. You obeyed, trying to tiptoe over the floor, and followed him into your study. There the stranger pointed to your work table and ordered you to sit down. Between the folders and bundles of quarto sheets, you spotted a fat, brightly shining pen, at least as long as a night on the road. Pick it up, he ordered, and write down everything I tell you without stopping. You obeyed, filled with fear and reverence, and he began to dictate unfalteringly every period, comma, parenthesis, hyphen, question mark and blank space of the thirty-two fragments that make up this book so far. The young man levitated in the room and addressed you as easily from the floor as suspended in midair, reclining on an invisible carpet. Although immersed in the task of writing, you observed his strikingly transparent body: you could see his luminous heart and the marrow of his bones, like a white thread inside a glass ball. You even guessed at his thoughts—as he read yours—and sometimes you overtook his dictation, anticipating the sentence that he was going to inspire in you. It was a laborious task, but you experienced no fatigue. The fragrant immediacy of his presence imbued your spirit with a gentle feeling of relief and security. All night long you composed the book in a delightful state of rapture. At daybreak, as the brow of dawn gleamed over the slate roofs, the messenger bowed farewell and faded into the diaphanous air with the speed of one of Scheherazade's characters in the chambers of the Abbasid caliph. You returned to your room and found your wife curled up asleep. As you settled down by her side, she woke up. When she saw you so excited and happy, she wanted to know why. You told her what had happened. Obviously giving no credence to what she heard, she advised you to go to bed and rest for a few hours so as to make up the lost sleep. But you wanted to telephone the friend who typed out your manuscripts, to hand him everything you had taken down from the angelic dictation.

Are you crazy? she asked. He'll think you're out of your mind. He'll laugh himself silly! Who'll ever believe that you wrote the book in one sitting, during a single night? Don't you realize he'll say you're telling him a cock-and-bull story?

In order to convince her that it was no dream, you went to your office to collect and show her proof of everything you'd done. It was only then you were puzzled to notice—in a state of confusion that Ibn Arabi confesses often took hold of him—that the resplendent pen had vanished and that the previous thirty-two fragments had been typed out.

The one you had added by hand was in reality an idiosyncratic adaptation of *The Book of the Ascent of the Prophet,* translated by order of Alfonso the Wise and used by Dante in the construction of his *Comedy!*

34

Afterwards, fatally after what had happened, he looked back, first alone, then with his wife, for the telltale signs of imminent departure, the symptoms of exodus. He recalled her sitting by the low table in his old study smiling trustingly just as in the photograph I'm looking at now as she took out one of her Gauloises Bleues or stubbed it out carefully in the improvised ashtray. They were talking about the *Comedy* and its connections with Islamic mysticism. Already unknowingly hanging on the inexorable countdown of fragile heartbeats, she had read excitedly: *But my heart assumes all shapes: / the monk's cloister, the idols' shrine, / the gazelles' meadow, the pilgrim's Kaaba, / the tablets of the Torah, the text of the Koran. / I profess the creed of love / which, wherever it points the way, / will always be my faith and doctrine.* If the mantle of charity spans the whole of creation and if even the mineral realm—a community just like any other!—glorified Creation, hadn't Ibn Arabi rent the veils and limitations of Dante in his vision of the afterlife? He looked through the half-opened window at the slate roofs and the array of variegated clouds brightly colored by the sun with an emotion he hadn't properly understood, so immersed was he in the purely literary dimension of the conversation. Then, suddenly, she had talked calmly about the violence of the universe. Not of the tiny planet where they lived but the immeasurable violence of the Cosmos: fiery stars emitting lethal rays; cold, dead stars; novas diffusing radioactive particles; quasars irradiating fabulous, incomprehensible energy; spiral, galactic nebula; black holes whose gravitational pull sucks into a swirling vortex the celestial bodies that have strayed into their vicinity. The fantastic, unimaginable, savage violence of stars situated millions of light years from our diminutive galaxy which consume a minimal part of their energy in the brief span of their existence then disappear in explosions of unheard-of proportions, giving rise to brutal collisions, staggeringly powerful radio waves, dizzy expansions, a chain of catastrophes in a world of sound and fury, that voracious world based on chaos, litigation, on the blind meeting of opposed forces described by Rojas in *La Celestina,* if you remember? She stopped. A question floated in the air he couldn't put into words: was there a particle of love and sweetness in that orb that was not prey to annihilation and terror? They both went silent and contemplated the ever more threatening and strange shapes of the clouds, their dark, serried ranks. It's going to rain, she said finally, getting up out of her chair.

(Was it then he gave her the *Spiritual Guide* by Molinos and issued an invitation to dinner on the following day?)

No, it was the same day, his wife replied. You'd spent the afternoon revising your translations and I asked her to stay on. I remember she wore a sweater and jeans and the gold chain she's wearing in the photo.

Did anything in her behavior and words catch their attention? They scratched around, excavated memories of that night, conversations with the other guests, references to literature and film, not noticing that an invisible presence, crouched down behind them, was witness to the scene, was taking possession of her body, endowing her forever in front of her friends with a fresh, enduring youthfulness.

(Nothing led you to suspect the abrupt end or imminent passing over to subtlety.)

When we said good-bye, she asked you for a book, which you fetched from the study.

(His wife was right: it was then that you lent her the *Guide* and for the last time kissed her on the cheek opposite the door to the elevator.)

35

Finally freed of the oppressive attentions of the Lady with the Parasol, you can roam at will, wander through the immensity of the heavens, check the detail of what's recorded in your copy of the *Miradj* or *Ascent.* You travel alone as on Earth, off the tourist routes with their air-conditioned buses, piped music, prerecorded commentaries and official polyglot guides. Infatuated by your eschatological reading, you halt the flight and levitation of your pen to lose yourself in the vision of angels of light, of exuberantly green birds. Prophets seated on radiant chairs, their heads wrapped in the purest, transparent cloth, spirits of fire, pupils that tremble seventy thousand times a day from fear of God, dazzlingly beautiful eyelashes the size of rainbows. Dulcet-toned muezzins summon the blessed souls to prayer and myriads of creatures noisily converge and proclaim the Uniqueness of the Deity to the compass of the winds. Immersed among them, you examine the slender, narrow bridge, subtler than a hair or the sharpest edge of a sword along which anxious souls walk balancing so as not to fall into the abysses of Gehenna. You run your eyes over the pages of the book trying to imagine angels with seventy thousand heads, each with seventy thousand faces and each of these with seventy thousand eyes, like the microscopic studies of the polarization of diverse substances, their fantastic, luminous refractions a visual apotheosis of disturbing beauty. Astray in an infinity of landscapes, you make out three familiar figures, seated around a table on a professorial dais, as if marooned on a desert island. You get closer to them and see it's George Sand, the politicologist and the psychoanalyst, still locked in their opposing theories, though nobody hangs on their words or pays them any attention. The lean-featured youth, wrapped in a threadbare djellaba and wearing an impish cap who was smoking a pipe of kef crouched by the door to the baths, is now holding them, dais and all, in the hollow of his cupped palms, smiling as cheerfully as a child who's gotten hold of a bird's nest. Is he protecting them from some danger? Will he blow on them, scatter them like chaff? Or is he about to wake up in his shack in Riad Ezzitun and disclose to the Cerberus of the baths the extraordinary contents of his dream?

Will you put in an appearance there?

One question torments you: Who will be the dreamer and who the dreamed?

36

He seized the bull by the horns, caught the plane by the skin of his teeth, flew to Cairo. The journey was a short dream allowing him to contemplate the insignificance of the world, a tiny mustard seed in the palm of the hand. When he arrived, everything happened the way the woman at the Accounts Tribunal had said it would. Among the police and inspectors responsible for vetting travelers he immediately spotted the youth from the baths glowing in a gentle halo. He noticed how he passed through their bodies without hurting them or being noticed by the owners. He decided to follow in his footsteps, copy his every act, put his feet where his had been. He had scarcely lifted his sole from one spot than he immediately pressed his own sole down into it, avoiding the checkpoints one by one, so nobody stamped his passport or registered his entry. Like a sluggish, stealthy saurian, a gleaming black taxi waited opposite the terminal and drove off as soon as they got in. They swiftly crossed a city deserted as in the moments before the breaking of the fast of Ramadan, passed no cars, stopped at no traffic lights. The driver laughed, whistled, gritted his teeth, emitted guttural sounds, wheezed, as if possessed by some anarchic, jovial inspiration. Did he at least know where he was driving them? Neither the young messenger nor he had exchanged a word or mentioned any destination; but the charioteer—he preferred to call him that—apparently knew the road well, was happy with the mission he was carrying out, absorbed in his nighttime rampage and the intensity of his enjoyment. Were they both in the presence of a subtle body from the barzakh or an expression of epiphany? In vain he tried to catch a glimpse of his face in the blind rearview mirror: the turban that wreathed his head shielded him from nosy stares. Did he possess the gift of speech or only that register of raw sounds given to someone wounded by the vision of beatitude or the ecstasy of penetration? The vehicle glided enigmatically between the mausoleums of Qait Bey, passed on its left the crossing to the sacred mountain of Mukattam, skirted the back gates and walls of the Citadel, descended towards Bab al Kharafa, and finally entered the outer wall of the City of the Dead. The moon did not light up the stelas or memorial stones on the graves, the striated domes of the mausoleums or the dusty streets next to the mosque of Imam Chafaai. He realized that the charioteer's dry, intermittent moans were quickening, as he twisted to the right along a route he himself had traveled so often, in reality and dream, towards the pantheon where he had slept on his previous stay. He recognized it in spite of the deep shadows, and tested the little gate the old man bolted so carefully. It wasn't locked! He pushed it open, then pulled it to after him. Messenger and charioteer abandoned him: he heard the car start up and furtively move away. Quietly he slipped past the cubbyhole where the guard harbored a devil down a well. Had the old man taken the elementary precaution of sliding the bolt or did he have a surprise in store for his guest and his mischievous, light-footed escort? He proceeded as far as the steps and entrance to the mausoleum, gently pushed the door, blindly searched for the guard's mattress next to the solid stone slab of the vault. The old man was there in his usual place, evident in his fitful breathing. He was getting ready to lie beside him when he heard an imperious voice ordering him to close the pantheon. He jumped to obey while in the dark, silent recesses he tried to locate the microphone or loudspeaker whence it came. Suddenly, a television screen lit up.

37

Lying comfortably in your tomb, like a corpse,

(who closed your eyelids, plugged your ears and nostrils with cotton, tied up your feet and jaws with tape, crossed your hands over your chest, and leaned your body to the right towards the qibla?)

you behold images of ruin and desolation: blackened brick walls, tottering facades, a mess of telephone and electrical cables, enormous craters opened up by bombs, truncated chimneys billowing malevolent yellow smoke. The camera seems to enjoy lingering on shots of apocalyptic fire, sulphurous stones, wells vomiting flames against a black, incinerating sun, the day gradually darkening, black, opaque clouds, razor-sharp lights shooting up from the ground, an artificial night of terror. Does the barren wind blow, cruel and harsh like a woman who can bear no children? No, the voice will say, these are not illustrations by Doré or paintings by Bosch. Don't search the cantos of the *Inferno* or the descriptions in the *Miradj!* Nakir and Munkar laugh during the brief dazzling scenes on the screen. Look, look what a good job you have done! Why do we need to repeat your inventiveness? Bonfires, millions of bonfires of every shape and size! Sinuous, pointed flames, craters of red sulphur, creatures melted down, deformed, flaccid bodies, women and children burning like carded wool! Dante's nine circles and the seven Gehennas from *The Book of the Ascent* and the many varieties of the damned to be found there! But you have mixed up the innocent and the criminal, punished the first and garlanded the second with laurels! Take a look at the smug assembly of the fathers of ballistic missiles with chemical and nuclear warheads, of decompression bombs and the elegant science of extermination; at the manufacturers and experts, designers of clean, smart weaponry, laser-guided with optic-fiber targeting! They and the pilots who launch them, sowing death with the indifference of the Fates, will endure a special torture, unknown to the authors in whose work you are immersed! Eternally piloting one of those invisible bombers undetectable by radar and clinically aiming at an impersonal, distant objective on the orders of High Command, but not noticing that their lethal burden is heading toward their own home, no less: that's right, toward their home and beloved family whose photo they carry in their wallet or stick on the flight control panel, towards the sweet, smiling faces of their children and better halves! Gazing, powerless and in despair, at the terror-stricken faces, convulsed limbs, mouths opened to emit futile howls before they're destroyed and mangled by their perfect, precise weaponry. A scene lasting seconds, but interminable seconds that will be reproduced trillions of times until the Day of Judgment!

Nakir and Munkar's guffaws resound round the vault and the echo lingers on while the television repeats its scenes of tenderness and horror, peace and annihilation, implacably punishing, they say, the fundamentalists of technoscience.

The film has ended and the pantheon is in darkness. Anxious, afraid they'll leave you in limbo without submitting you to the necessary examination, you'll ask, in a raised voice, what they've decided to do with you: you have come expressly to find out, you want to know your destiny, to leave quarantine once and for all!

The screen lights up again and you'll read the message meant for you: THIS IS ONLY A VISION. WE'LL BE WAITING FOR YOU HERE WHEN YOU REALLY DIE.

As you throw off sleep, you'll hear at your side the old man's muffled, peaceful snores.

38

The war was ending, the diasporas beginning. From his house he watched the sad caravan of fugitives, his nose pressed against windowpanes steamed up by harsh, seasonal weather. First motorbikes and sidecars laden with belongings and families; then vehicles drawn by animals; finally the endless procession of women and men stiff with cold, tired out by their long march: old people, helpless and exhausted, mothers, their children tied on their backs, close to collapse. Worn out they stopped to cry, relieve themselves, or beg a piece of bread, a bowl of soup from the patriots in disorderly retreat. Broken-down cars and motorbikes, dead animals, mattresses and bundles lay by the roadside abandoned in the desperate flight to the mountains. Horror at the bombing raids and the army's brutal repression emptied their minds, turned them into a miserable, terrified flock, a trampled, scattering line of ants. Did the young boy carrying his younger brother or the old man with the faint, grief-stricken silhouette of a wife on his back know where they were heading or what welcome was being prepared? Were they going to be let in by frontier guards, beaten back by gun butts, herded behind barbed wire fences in inhospitable camps, or given back to the enemy without a second thought? Nobody knew or even seemed to pose the question. The magnitude of the disaster had swept everything away, left them naked and helpless in another repetition of their cruel, primitive history: panic, pure instinct for survival, the look of a hunted animal flickering in their eyes, disbelief, the glazed shock of someone dying at the hands of an anonymous slaughterer or as a sacrificial offering in some millennial ritual.

Crouched down in his tiny kingdom, he was witnessing the exodus of whole peoples, without guides or leaders, partings of the Red Sea or life-bringing Moses: no illusion of a Promised Land at the end of their confused, headlong flight! Were they Kurdish survivors of Halabja, Dahuk, or Mosul, or simply fellow citizens of his who fifty-two years earlier had passed through the Catalan village where he lived as a refugee, dirty and ragged like that, leaving behind a trail of corpses and excrement? Did the images shown on the television news relate to events after forty days of airborne hell or unearth reminiscences buried in his memory of somber civil war?

He was undecided, was still undecided.

For who was really writing that page? The writer in his sixties bent over his desk or the ignorant child who for the first time in his life saw a dream destroyed, a hope abruptly dashed?

39

Do you realize? she said. We're already at the end of the quarantine. One more day, one more chapter and I'll leave you, far from the barzakh, forever faded into subtlety, until the Great Resurrection foretold. She looked at you sadly from the photo, with a fleeting smile that is both anxious and fragile, as in the days when she came to your old study with her translations and you talked of Cervantes and Rojas, of Dante and Ibn Arabi. Your unexpected encounter after her passage had helped her greatly, she said: the burden of the unformulated, of everything unexpressed in the crass world and stored in her inner self, so much useless ink in the inkwell prevented her from fully enjoying her new state. Hadn't she totally cast off the sensuous world, as she believed, or was it the eye of your imagination that had only managed to represent her in that previous form and appearance? Had the accumulation of anachronisms, absurdities, mutations of space and time throughout your wanderings existed in material reality or did they obey your internalized readings of Ibn Arabi? Unable to reply with any certainty, beset by doubts, you could only scrutinize her, while she or her shade remained entranced by the perspective of garret rooftops, the bilious green dome of the Opéra and the distant, contrasting silhouettes of the skyscrapers of La Défense.

Had the moment for farewells arrived? You watched

her get up out of her seat and ask if smoke still upset you. Just one Gauloise Bleue, my last one, she added. Following the ritual you pushed the improvised ashtray in her direction and sat cowed by the desk, covered with notes and sheets of paper.

Was she wearing a sweater and jeans as on the night when she had dinner with you after which you never saw her again? You tried not to look at her.

Write, keep writing about me, you heard. Only your interest and the interest of those who read you can continue to keep me alive!

40

All that had happened during my short-lived agony. When I finished the book, I got up from the bed where I was lying unnoticed by anyone, put on my only remaining striped suit, tidied the knot of an old, forgotten tie, and took a bus to the Tribunal. I asked the porter and he pointed me to the elevator to the seventh floor, to the meeting place for those summoned to quarantine. When I arrived, it was empty, and following the concierge's advice I rapped on the solid office door to the interrogation room where a small gold plate displayed the names of Nakir and Munkar.